"A dramatic and heart-rending love story."

Georgina Hanratty in *Publishing News*

"Incredibly accomplished...a captivating tale of love, tragedy, immense danger and separation."

Louise Weir, www.lovereading4kids.co.uk

"Pauline Francis is masterful at turning dusty history into something alive & relevant...astonishingly good."

Claudia Mody, Waterstones

Pauline Francis

For David

First published in the UK in 2008 by Usborne Publishing Ltd., Usborne House, 83-85 Saffron Hill, London EC1N 8RT, England. www.usborne.com

Maps illustrated by Ian McNee.

A CIP catalogue record for this book is available from the British Library.

UK ISBN 9780746081129 First published in America in 2010. AE
American ISBN 9780794527563

FMAMJJASOND/10 94161
Printed in Yeovil, Somerset, UK.

"But true love is a durable fire
In the mind ever burning..."

Sir Walter Raleigh

To the Edge of the World

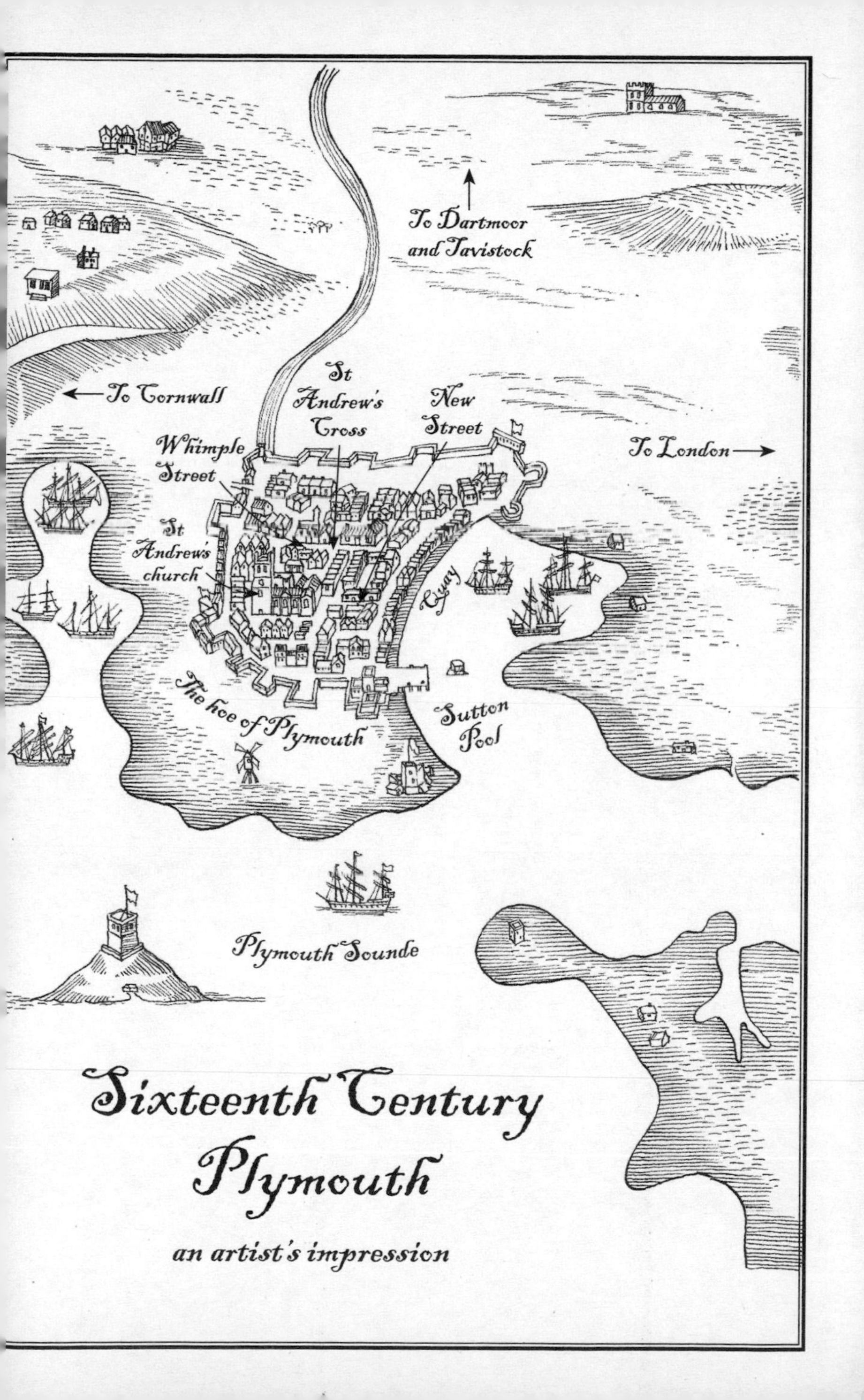
To Dartmoor
and Tavistock
To Cornwall
St
Andrew's
Cross
New
Street
To London
Whimple
Street
St
Andrew's
church
Quay
The hoe of Plymouth
Sutton
Pool
Plymouth Sounde
Sixteenth Century
Plymouth
an artist's impression

Secota, The Americas, 1586

Flames light the length of my mother's body and lick around her slender neck. Above her, leaves shrivel and branches blacken. Pale men, their armor glinting, swing their fire torches against the early sunrise.

What have they done?

Behind her, flames leap from the roof of our house. On the steps, painted pots shatter in the heat. I run toward her, calling for my cousin. My mother has not made a sound until she hears my voice. Then she screams at me to stay away.

I stand still, breathing in the scent of her burning flesh, crying out until a pale man, his cruel eyes taunting between beard and helmet, drags me away. He pulls me down to the creek and throws me into a boat full of pale men. Some pull the oars. Others level their muskets toward the bank, where my cousin Seekanauk stands and calls my name.

Seekanauk dives. The man sitting next to me fires his musket, sending out sparks of fire and hurting my ears, and I dare not look at the water. I fix my eyes on my village, Secota, half-hidden in the smoke, until we round the headland, where the fishing boats rock in our wash. I cannot take in what I have seen, what my father has not seen because he is away hunting.

Who are these men? Where are they taking me?

Salt from the spray stiffens my skin as I watch the smoke curl into the dawn. My father will come for me. When he returns from the hunt, he will ask our chief, Manchese, to let him fetch his canoe and find us.

Wingina, chief of all the village chiefs, welcomed the pale men when they came across the great salt water, and permitted them to build a fort on one of our islands. When they came to Secota, they came in peace with gifts of gaudy glass and a metal cooking pot. One of their men marveled so much at our corn and copper that he painted pictures of us. He laughed when he told me his name. Not all pale people are called White he said. His work was to show my land to his people across the sea.

I learned to speak his tongue so well that I helped to interpret for the other pale people. It suited me, because I do not like women's work: softening the deerskin to stitch into skirts, pounding the corn into flour.

But my father changed. His bright eyes darkened. He cursed the pale men because they brought a spotted sickness that killed Seekanauk's father and sister. *Keep away from them, Nadie,* he said. *They want to take our women to breathe life back into themselves. They are bloodless. Their hair hangs from their faces. They foul the water that we drink. What creature would do that?*

We skirt my land all day. The rattle of the oars startles the seabirds. The men curse as they slap mud. One of them offers me a green fruit, and I take it for its juice because my throat is dry. At last, I see Roanoke Island on my right, the last island inhabited by the Secotan people before the great salt water that stretches to the horizon.

On the mainland, opposite Roanoke Island, is the village of Desamonquepeuc. This is where Wingina lives. I respect him, not just because he is the great chief of all the village chiefs, but because he is intelligent. He does not believe that the pale men have come back from the dead. They eat and drink too much for that, he laughs.

My heart lifts as we come to shore. *He* will punish the pale people for what they have done today.

There are more pale men waiting for us, wild-eyed and shooting fire into the air as I am pushed from the boat. I think this is their greeting, for two men in silver helmets come from the trees, carrying Wingina. How peaceful he looks as he stares at the sky. Turkey feathers decorate his hair, turkey claws hang from his ears. Clay splashes his forehead and face like dried blood. Copper and pearls coil around his neck and down the lion skin wrapped around his body.

I kneel. The men halt in front of me, laughing as they tip him from their shoulders, laughing as Wingina's head rolls onto the sand, his ragged neck soon gritted with fine shells. The seabirds shriek back at me. I beg the gods in the Upper World to receive him; I ask my mother to care for him.

Then the sky and the sea tilt, green and gray, into a darkness so deep that even the shadows disappear.

Plymouth, England, 1586

Tom

It's too hot to hammer the horseshoes in the forge.

I open the door and let the smoke find its way into the street. I've never been so busy, for the harvest has been cut early and the plough horses have had to be shod many times. I glance at the second anvil, closer to the fire, the one that my father used. I miss the rhythm of his hammer with mine.

From the doorway, further down the steep street, I can see Abigail in front of her father's shop. Even her pale face is scarlet.

Not a breath of wind to bring in the ship.

I saw it last night from the tavern steps, settling on the horizon like a giant seabird, sails glinting under the harvest moon. Although I know the name of every ship – and every famous seaman that sails in and out of the harbor, the sight of the sea makes me shudder. How can men set sail, not knowing whether a storm will sink them in a squall?

I like the walls of Plymouth. I like belonging to a family of blacksmiths that's worked here as far back as anybody can remember.

But that waiting ship's brought a ripple of excitement. It's part of Sir Francis Drake's fleet straggling back across the great ocean from the New World, where it rescued a small English colony from a place called Virginia.

The seamen from the first ship told us in the tavern that this one carries a young girl from Virginia with breasts as big as ale jugs, skin as dark as burned wood, wearing a deerskin that hardly covers that private part of her – and enough copper to make a kettle.

Not a breath of air. I pray for the wind to come, to bring us the cargo we all want to see.

Every time I open my eyes, I see the shifting flames of a candle. I shrink away from its heat, away from the tangled hair on the face of the man who is holding it.

I *know* him. Master John White, the man who came to Secota to paint pictures of my people.

Now words pour from his mouth. I understand that I am on a ship sailing to his land, England – to a town called Plymouth – and that we have already sailed too far to turn back. His eyes brim with tears as he tells me. But no words come to me, either in his tongue or in mine.

I refuse to leave that little room, sliced by gray light from chinks in the wood. And I refuse to leave the bench where I lie to look through them. Master White brings the food of my land to tempt me: corn, beans and berries. Sometimes, another man comes with him, soothing me in my tongue, for he speaks it well. He is Master Hariot, a young man who sailed with Master White, who smokes tobacco in a pipe as our men do.

"*She* will do more for Raleigh's next colony than all your paintings, John," he says. "She is young and beautiful and pure – and ready for the taking, just like Virginia. *She* will persuade people to come with us next time. Yes, Sir Walter Raleigh will be pleased. She will do much to make up for the disappointment of abandoning Virginia."

Master White clenches his fists. "You fool, Thomas! What have you done? You have taken her from everything she has ever known – dashing our future hopes and dreams in a moment of foolishness. How will her people ever forgive us? How will we ever be able to go back?"

If you do not speak, people forget that you can hear. In this way, I learn that the pale people are planning to live again in my land, that they will take our wood to build new ships, that they will search for copper and gold, that they will stop the Spanish people from moving north to take my land, as they have already done in Florida.

Let them think I am an ignorant savage.

I press my face against the gaps in the wood. Sea spray stings my eyes. No land beckons.

I lie down once more.

I count forty more days on that ship until the days cool – forty days of drizzling mists and howling winds. Then the sun comes back, lighting a path along the sea, and through my wooden world. Above my head, I hear running feet and rough voices calling out words I do not know.

Master White coaxes me from my lair. We climb a flight of wooden stairs and step into daylight, where water rises and falls around me. Gray smudges the horizon and seabirds squawk over our heads.

The world does not end at the horizon, my mother used to whisper. But I hoped that it did, for I was happy in my world, in my village perched between forest and creek, knowing that I was becoming beautiful by the way the young men looked at me. But when I was thirteen summers old, and restless, I stared out to sea with my mother, and we saw what we thought was an island floating past our creek, its treetops lost in billowing clouds.

But now I know that it was not an island. There are no leaves on those tall trees, only men – ragged and hairy – running up and down ropes, grabbing at white cloth, which slaps their faces. I am on a wooden ship, far bigger than any canoe that my people can build.

Master White stares at the sky, murmuring words I do not understand. Then he kneels on the tilting deck and clasps his hands, repeating words so melodious that tears come to my eyes. Some of the men leave their work to join us, and they call out "*Amen*".

My heart quietens. I follow Master White's eyes. That is where my mother and Wingina are, in the Upper World, where everything is pure and perfect. I want them to hear *me.* Stretching out my arms, I sing my own lament.

As the smudges sharpen to land, I glimpse a river snaking from the sea to the trees on the horizon. Men fish around us. Late summer sun reddens the water as we sail past a small island. My heart leaps.

Have we come back to Roanoke Island? *Has* Master White brought me home?

I shall see my father. I shall honor my mother's grave.

But stone towers guard the harbor here, holding huge chains that have been pulled back to let us enter. Houses, their stone walls gleaming, cling to a hill. A wide street twists up toward a building towering against the sunset. Tumbling down to the sea is a green hill, guarded by another stone building with four towers.

I look away, fearful.

Now I am certain of one thing. I am not in my land.

How can I live without my own people?

Tom

I run down to the quayside just as I am, hair blackened with soot and smoke, blacksmith's apron still tied around me. It seems that the whole of Plymouth has come to gawp. Every wall, every fishing boat, every warehouse window's crammed. My friends, Josiah and Walter, are clinging to the steps of the tavern. Only the fishermen, used to such sights, carry on their work.

Abigail squeezes next to me on the quayside wall. She caught up with me at the bottom of the lane, leaving her father to mind the bread ovens. We wait an age in a cool sea mist, until a cannon booms from Drake's ship anchoring in Sutton Pool. As the small boats approach the quay, a piper plays his welcome.

A man of about forty, bearded and his cap brightly feathered, jumps from the first boat, and pushes a boy up the steps. "Run, boy!" he shouts, his voice frantic. "Bring the Reverend Newton here at once! *Run!*"

The boy disappears into the gloom of New Street like somebody with an attack of the flux. The man waits, impatient, as the seamen around him untie the sacks they've brought with them.

We crane our necks.

One of them holds up the head of a long-beaked bird, with a baggy pouch hanging underneath. Another pulls out a curving brown shell and one of the ship's boys crawls with it on his back. The children clap.

But that wasn't the cargo we'd come to see.

The shout goes up: "Let's see the little Indian girl!"

The mist clears, revealing the strangest boat we've ever seen – a long tree trunk, hollowed out, its sides patterned black. At its prow stands a girl of about fourteen or fifteen, dark eyes peering through a fringe of black hair, skin as dark as the horse I shod yesterday. Her hair is coiled back, showing a blue and yellow tattoo twisting from her neck to her breasts, which are partly covered with bone and pearl necklaces. A deerskin hardly covers her womanhood. Her tiny feet are shod in leather. Copper glints at her ears.

My mouth hangs open. The houses, the Hoe, the harbor: all slip away from me in that moment.

Now a young man at the back of the boat pushes her up the steps. He bows to the crowd. "My name is Thomas Hariot," he shouts, "returned, as you know, from the New World, sent there by Her Majesty, Queen Elizabeth, charged with the duty of the exploration of the territory of Virginia. Feast your eyes, people of Plymouth." He touches the girl's arm. He revolts me, the way he paws her like a buyer at a horse fair. "She is called Nadie, the wise one...wise enough to come and look at our world." He picks up the turtle shell. "Her people believe the earth lies on a turtle shell hanging beneath the sky. Her land is as beautiful as she is, as scented as a summer garden, trees taller than your church tower...

walnuts as big as eggs...exotic fruits for the picking, and..."

Abigail shudders. "She's ugly," she whispers. "Big nose and small eyes. Ugh! And so black..."

"Hold your tongue, Abigail," I say. "You're so pale she'll think you're a ghost come to gawp."

The women nearest to Nadie pull their children away, but a man touches the tattoo on her neck. "Let's see where the vine leads us," he calls. "To a juicy fruit, I bet."

The man with the bright feather in his cap takes off his cloak and wraps it around her shoulders. "You shall *not* parade her like a wild animal, Hariot. Henry Newton will care for her until I can take her back to Virginia – God and the Queen willing."

As he speaks, the Reverend is parting the crowd. "What have you done now, John?" he asks.

"Nothing, Henry, and that is the problem."

They whisper, as we grow impatient. The girl called Nadie stares ahead, her eyes glazed with terror. The Reverend grasps Master Hariot's arm. "Shame on you, Thomas Hariot! *You* of all people! A man educated at

Oxford University, one of the best scientific minds in England...to snatch a child from her home. May God forgive you, sir."

"I am doing it for England," Hariot replies, scowling, "and for our Queen. We must colonize the New World if our country is to be rich...if we are to get the better of Spain." He reaches for Nadie. "Give her to me, John."

And so they quarrel, until Nadie lets out a scream that startles the seabirds. Now the tide turns. The people of Plymouth raise their fists to Hariot, and some of the children pelt him with stones. Only then does he let her go, ordering the men to fill the sacks again. Then he enters the tavern to drown his sorrows.

They lead Nadie away. I want to understand what she's saying, for the terror in her voice sickens me.

Hasn't Master Hariot noticed her swollen eyelids, the sores at the corners of her mouth, the twitching skin of a terrified creature?

I want to protect her.

But, to my shame, I admit that, like all the men around me, I wonder what it would be like to taste such an exotic fruit.

I sink my teeth into the hand that holds me. Master White does not fuss or flinch. He clutches me to him, tears wetting his face, repeating, "He should not have brought you here, poor child."

The waterside is choked with pale people. I see pale women for the first time: their dresses, white at the neck and wrists, hide their bodies. Caps cover their hair.

As I set foot in this new world, even the dogs stop barking. People press close, trying to touch me, releasing a wave of stinking sweat. A man spits on my skin and rubs hard.

Am I in a world of bad spirits who want to kill me? Am I in *popogusso*, the pit of hell, where all is confusion and chaos?

I refuse to move.

"Can you see that stone house?" Master White whispers. "The one by the tower? The Reverend Henry Newton – he is like your *shaman* – lives there. He is a friend of mine. No harm will come to you, I promise."

He half-carries, half-drags me from the waterside: a biting, kicking creature, as wild as the pale people fear.

A boy is standing on the wall – his hair and skin as brown as mine, wearing a leather apron as my people do. His arms and body are short and strong, like a tree that has been lopped and grown sideways. I greet him in my tongue, but he raises his eyebrows, puzzled, and I see that his eyes are green, and I blush at my mistake.

The girl next to him, with skin and hair as pale as the moon, laughs.

But he does not laugh with her.

✲ ✲ ✲

The fire of my nightmares keeps me in a fever. But when my cheeks cool, I see a young woman sitting by my bed, her hands clasped, her eyes closed. Even in repose, her face is worried, the corners of her eyes already crinkling, although she cannot be much older than I. She wears a brown dress, with white at the neck. A white cap hides most of her hair, except for a dark curl which has fallen onto her forehead as she leans forward.

When she sees that I am awake, she bathes my face, and tells me that her name is Hester. Then she goes to fetch food for me.

Why am I alone? In Secota, we are only left alone when we have our loss of blood each moon. Only then do we not work and food is brought to us. But I have had no such blood since I left my land.

Light floods the room through two large windows. One gives me sight of the harbor, now empty of the ship that brought me. The other shows me a garden full of trees and flowers, with blue-gray hills beyond. I sniff. No deerskins, no reed mats, no bear grease – only a smell like the flowers in the forest, and I like it.

Then terror takes hold of me. On the wall hangs a man, naked except for a cloth around his waist. Blood flows from his hands and feet where he has been tied to a piece of wood.

I am crying when Hester comes back. "It is a painting, Nadie, like the ones Master White did of your village. This man is the Son of our God. He died on that wooden cross, but He came to life again. Let Him comfort you in your grief."

That night, the wind moans and the sea laps the waterside. But above the sounds, I hear the shouts of my people, hear my mother scream at me to stay away as flames light her body. I push my hand into my mouth, trying not to cry out, trying to think instead of the brown-skinned boy who did not look away.

I sit up and glimpse the sea at the foot of the tumbling street. My heart lifts at the sight of it – at the sight of my way back. Then I close the wooden shutter and settle to sleep.

How can I wait for Master White's ship to take me

home? These people are my enemies. They have killed and burned.

I want to go back to Secota *now.*

Tom

I'm not one for the steady flame. I'm quick to flare, though quick to cool. They say that you can tell how many years a man will live by the wrinkles on his forehead, so I don't stay angry for long. But I hammered on the anvil with the fury of a madman when I was back in the forge, hitting my fingers although I didn't feel the pain.

Nadie had reared and bucked like a frightened horse.

Master Hariot's spitting blood when he brings his musket to me. With a tongue still loosened by ale, he boasts that he must make his way to London to write his report for the Queen, in which he will persuade her to set up a new colony in Virginia. And he must do this without his prize exhibit, Nadie, for he can't take her to London now.

My anger rises. I wait until I've repaired the musket catch before I dare speak. "You shouldn't have taken her from her family, sir." I step back, fearing that he'll cuff me.

"It is none of your business, blacksmith boy, but since you have poked your nose in, I shall tell you. I was doing her a favor. By God, her world *is* beautiful. But it is a hard life for its women. They lose their beauty quickly, planting and cutting, cooking and childbearing. Nadie spoke English so well that—"

"You took her as a curiosity, because it suited you," I cut in. "Your men burned her village...and her mother. It's common knowledge already."

"I sent fools to fetch her. When they could not find Nadie that morning, they thought her people were hiding her. They decided to teach them a lesson..."

He stops, suddenly aware of what he's saying. He throws a coin to the ground, much more than the job's worth. "Keep your silence, boy! By God, it's as dark as a Virginian forest in here."

"You can't have sun shining on the metal, sir. I need to see how red-hot it is when…"

But he's not listening. He's making his way to the quayside, bound for Portsmouth – and then to London – with all his treasures except one.

Toward dusk, I dampen down the fire, touch my tools twice for luck as I do every night, and make my way along the lane that skirts the garden of the vicarage, the one we all call Back Lane. It's my favorite walk in this season: the leaves already coloring and men working in the fields by the light of the moon. I like the way men and horses work together – long into the night to cut corn and plough for the next harvest.

Every window at the vicarage is shuttered. I pick up an apple and watch for a long time. Nadie's unsettled me in a way that I don't understand.

Then I make my way to the tavern, eager to learn more about the exotic fruit in our midst.

I run my fingers along my bony hips, along my shoulder blades, which stick out like a bird's wings. My tattoos have wrinkled. My breasts have shrunk. Master Hariot will not want to parade me now. His exotic bird has flown.

Hunger bites deep, for I refuse the food that Hester brings. Silver tongues lick my feverish mind, scattering in my head like sizzling tobacco powder in the flames, burning into my brain and telling me to go home. I see colors cascading from ceiling to floor. Red the color of the maple tree; yellow the color of sunflowers, and green the color of new corn leaves. Then they flash silver and gold, showering sparks inside my head.

I can do *anything* I want. I am as light as a feather.

I can go home now.

I tiptoe downstairs, creeping through the kitchen to unbolt the door.

My nightshift billows like a ship's sail as I run down to the waterside. Houses and shops and ships blur. I pass women who mock me with their painted mouths, past men relieving themselves in the water, beating each other with their fists, sprawling at my feet.

Popogusso. The pit of hell, where all is chaos and confusion.

Seabirds swoop around me. I sniff salt and stale tobacco. A thousand horses pound through my head. Dazzling light spirals toward the sky, and I stretch out my arms. Whether the light is in my head or from the moon, I can no longer tell, but it sharpens into the piercing eyes of an eagle, its wings wide open.

"Mighty Thunderbird that lives between earth and sky," I call. "Take me home, or to my mother."

I close my eyes, swaying at the waterside, waiting to feel the rush of air. But sweaty hands grip my arms, and a boy's voice whispers, "Hello, my black beauty! What's thee doing out here all alone?" He pushes me against a rough wall, his stinking lips pressed against mine, his hands fumbling under my nightshift. "Only whores go out in the dark." I recognize the menace in his voice, although I do not understand the word *whore.* "White shift aping white skin!" he shouts.

Another voice hisses from the tavern doorway. "There's no sport here, Walter. Leave her."

"But it's the little black Indian maid, Tom."

The boy called Tom leads me toward the fire torch on the wall and puts his hand against mine. "She's brown, not black, you dolt. And her name's Nadie."

My heart quickens, not just because he knows my name, but because he is the boy on the waterside wall, the one who did not look away, although his hair is no longer black, but the color of corn, of a sunflower, of the sun itself.

"He doesn't know any better, Nadie." His words roll deep in his throat. "He's never seen a maiden with brown skin before." He cuffs Walter lightly. "Now be off with you before I tan your hide." Tom turns to me. "He's a good lad at heart, and he'll soon get used to the sight of you." He puts out his hand to touch the copper at my ears. "I'd give anything to work such a metal," he whispers.

I curse him then, and run back to the waterside, kicking out as he tries to stop me. Then he whispers soft words like pattering rain, and when he leads me away, fire runs through my body. "Promise you'll never come out alone at nightfall," he says. I can hear his tongue hissing against his front teeth.

"I want to go home."

"Which home is that?" he asks. But there is no malice in his voice.

Now rain darkens the sea. I let Tom take me to Whimple Street. Once more, I am safely delivered into the arms of Henry and Hester.

And when I wake up the next morning, I drink the milk and honey that Hester brings me, and the lights in my head disappear.

Tom

I curse myself for touching her earrings. It's the first rule of handling a nervous horse. Never make a sudden move. It's the only way to win its trust. She was skin and bone when I held her and as highly strung as a young filly – and as dangerous as the mare that killed my father this last spring.

That night was a dark one, wet with squalls, and the traveler who banged at our door boasted that he'd whipped his mare all the way from Dartmoor. He wanted to reach the town before last light. A blacksmith's forge invites such talk. Men spill their secrets in the firelight, as they do in the alehouse.

My father was keen to shut up shop. But travelers often come late because we're close to the city gate and the road stretching north to the moors – and because our horseshoes are the best in Plymouth. Horses stand still for me. I'm young and nimble-handed, and I only have to touch their knee and they lift their hoof. I know their needs better than any stable boy.

But my father was stubborn that night. Exhausted, he insisted on doing the work himself, insisted that I pump the bellows for the fire. The mare was overtired, too. That's when they're most dangerous. She wouldn't stand still for him, but reared as he lifted the hoof that had lost its shoe. The rider whipped her. My father let the hoof fall, shouting, "We'll have none of that in my forge!"

Startled, the mare kicked out.

My father's skull cracked. I heard him gasp as he fell and, if he wasn't already dead, the flagstones finished the job. The firelight caught his tools on the wall:

hammers and chisels, carefully crafted by his hands. He said that a craftsman's tools are only of use if they're made with love.

The mare bolted through the door, and its rider with it, letting in shafts of sunset. And in that moment, my life was shaped, as quickly as the metal in the fire.

To my shame, although I love my father dearly and miss him every day, I can't forgive him for dying before my apprenticeship was finished. It takes seven years of working for a master blacksmith to learn the blacksmith's trade. From the age of ten, I've spent six years puffing the bellows, stoking the fire, hammering and shaping the metal, all to become a master blacksmith like my father and his father before him. We Martyns come from a long line of blacksmiths.

A few months more and I'd have been earning five pounds a year.

He taught me the mysteries of the forge – for what? My mother can't afford to apprentice me to anybody else.

I'm still luckier than most, I know it. Whenever I work the metal, it's the same thrill: the race to shape the metal before it cools. Like him, I make my horseshoes with love. I earn enough to keep body and soul together. I don't have to brand the forehead of a thief or burn a hole through a beggar's ear lobe, like some smiths I know.

But it doesn't stop me dreaming of the day when I'll forge a rich man's firedogs or a fireback engraved with his coat of arms.

All because of a tormented horse.

If only he'd let me shoe her.

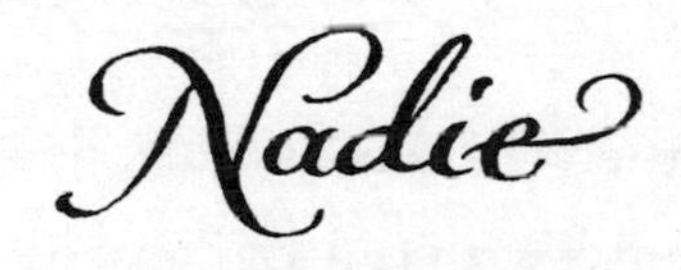

I want to dress, but it takes two days of washing before I am clean enough for Hester. I want to hate her, but I cannot, for she is kind to me.

It is not her fault, I repeat inside my head.

She covers my body with layers of soft cloth that soothe my skin, itchy from the weeks on the water. My new clothes please me. My dress, the color of my skin, except for the lace at the cuffs, pinches in my waist and pushes up my breasts. But I do not like the cap that holds back my fringe.

Hester touches my earrings. "Listen to me, Nadie. Chaste ladies do not wear such things, unless they are costly jewels. Let me remove them. *Please!*"

What does she mean?

"NO," I cry, and she takes away her hand. "Am I to be your slave?" I ask.

Hester shakes her head.

"Who am I, then?"

"You are Nadie," she says.

I prowl in the garden, whether the sky is blue or dripping rain. There are trees heavy with red and green fruit, some tamed and tied to the walls, some standing free. A lane winds behind the garden wall, bordering a stream. My people would bathe in such water, women upstream, men downstream, then gather around the fire to tell stories, to gossip.

The gray-blue hills beyond make me shudder.

"That is Dartmoor," Hester tells me. "It is always wild and windy up there. Even on the hottest day, the mist can suddenly come down and you dare not move for fear the bog will suck you in."

I look away. They remind me too much of the hills beyond Secota where the Mangoak live. They are a treacherous people, whom we fear, and whom we call the snakes who cannot be trusted. They spike their hair with the feathers of parrots and hummingbirds. They take captives to work their copper, and cut out the tongues of those who try to escape and hang them on a tree. We children called it the terror tree, and our parents used it as a threat to make us behave, to stop us straying from the village. And when the leaves fell at the time of our harvest, I imagined they were shriveled tongues.

But I do not tell Hester this. I do not think she could bear it.

There are so many rules.

I must learn to sew, not to drink when my mouth is full of food, not to pick my nails, not to pick my nose, to use a knife and spoon, to eat fish on Wednesdays, Fridays and Saturdays, to help the fishermen earn a living, to be silent when eating, to eat at a table with a man – and not to go out alone at nightfall.

The most difficult rule for me is to be on time. Here it is measured with clocks that chime in the parlor and on the church tower. Even when it is dark, the nightwatchman wakes me as he calls out the hour.

Master Henry works in the building with the tower, Saint Andrew's church. This is where he prays to his god, with most of the people of Plymouth, and where they make offerings of bread.

I refuse to go there. I am afraid of the great clanging that thunders from the tower. I am afraid they will force me up there, only to throw me to the ground again. Hester says that I will be safe and that God's love will calm me, as it did on the ship. So I go at last, clutching her arm as we cross the burying ground, so slowly that the church is almost full as we take our place on the wooden seat at the front.

People nudge each other as we pass. But Hester is right. The singing, the murmured talking, the music droning like swarming bees, the *amens*: all work their magic on me.

Master Henry, his hands clasped, his skin as pale as if the frost lies on it, glides past us, his black dress skimming the stone floor, and takes his place behind a glinting eagle. I have not noticed it until now.

The mighty Thunderbird. Has it come to take me home at last? Or has it come to take me to my mother? My eyes close. Henry almost sings his words:

"I was hungry and ye fed me, thirsty and ye gave me a drink; I was a stranger and ye received me in your home, naked and ye clothed me…"

His voice dies away. In my mind, I am seated on the Thunderbird's back, sun blinding me, high over a land that is not my island, nor this island. It is like no land I have seen: sunlit and serene. Wingina squats in the sunshine, his head thrown back, laughing, his face unlined as if he has shed the cares of the world. I laugh. My eyes seek out my mother. I search every face in that world of eternal sunshine. But I cannot see her.

Where is she? Panic chokes me. Has she gone to *popogusso*, to the pit of hell?

As the picture fades in my mind, grief chokes me, pressing down on me until I throw back my head and utter a shriek that echoes from stone to stone. Henry leans forward, his nose, as sharp as an arrowhead, almost piercing me.

"In the name of God, compose yourself!" he cries.

And Hester hushes me and hurries me outside.

Tom

She ran from the church like a bolting horse. I couldn't help her this time. It would have brought comment. I cursed myself for being afraid of what people might think, just as I'd cursed myself for touching the copper at her ears.

Abigail, who's sitting behind me, giggles. The Reverend calls for order as his congregation turns to gawp. He's enough to startle anybody – skin like a dead man's, eyes like blocks of ice peering down at her.

A man who lacks fire, unless he's speaking of God.

Why did he take Nadie into his home? To prove how godly he is and then remind her of it in front of all Plymouth?

I want to run after her. But I feel my dead father's hands tugging at my breeches.

One stifling summer's day, just before harvest, I was sitting in this same pew with my mother and father and my brother, Francis. I was about three years old, Francis four years older. A cannon boomed beyond the harbor and people began to leave the church for the quayside, all except a few pious souls who turned their back to the sea – including my father, who wouldn't let me go. He grasped the back of my breeches.

Not because he was pious, he told me later, but because he'd no time for Sir Francis Drake, who'd come back from a raid in the Caribbean islands, bringing so much loot that his ships couldn't carry it all.

His face darkened. "They had to leave the silver behind, son, so that they could carry the gold. He's nothing more than a common thief! I'd brand him, if it wasn't a waste of a good fire."

My mother went to watch. In her eyes, Sir Francis could do no wrong.

Now Abigail's scoffing as she leans forward to cup her hand around my ear. "The devil's made a good catch there," she whispers. "She's trouble. I can sniff it a mile off. Walter says she's got a tattoo on her left breast."

"Your brother should keep his mouth shut."

"Did she bewitch you with her strange spells on the quayside, Tom? The seamen say that her people offer their women, like we offer food. Is that what you want? 'Cos I won't lie with you until we're wed?"

I grip her hand. "You're not a fool, Abigail, so why say such foolish words? And don't speak of wedding me. I've never promised such a thing."

She shrugs me off and closes her eyes in prayer.

When the service's ended, I leave Abigail standing in the church porch with my mother, who calls after me to come back. On the Lord's Day, after church, Abigail and I usually walk with my mother on Plymouth Hoe. It's the only day drink doesn't pass her lips, except for the communion wine, and this walk seems to be the unspoken price I've got to pay – a short time when my mother can hope that I'll wed Abigail one day.

No, I've never refused that walk. And my mother's face always shines bright, as it did before my father died, as she dreams of the daughter she's never had. Francis was named after the great man himself, and I would have been named Judith if I'd been the living daughter my mother desired, for that was the name of one of Drake's ships. The daughter she longed for – my twin – died at birth, and she named me for that: Thomas, the twin. How could she have known then how difficult my name would be for somebody who lisps as I do?

I make my way to Back Lane. Even before I reach the wall of the vicarage garden, I hear the rooks cawing as they circle. Nadie's standing under an apple tree. Her cap lies on the grass, her fringe now long enough to cover her eyes. She shakes her hair like a horse shakes off summer flies. Her body trembles as her bare feet paw and stamp the ground. She calls out words I don't know, words that end with the click of her tongue as she stretches out her arms. Then she beats her body to her own rhythm. Round and round she whirls, never leaving the same patch of grass, tugging at her hair, giving cries that jolt her body and mine, her voice as raucous as the rooks.

The wild horse, before it's tamed.

Excitement grips me, so strong that I'm afraid, and my heartbeat quickens until it beats to her rhythm. My eyes glaze.

The church bells finish their peal, and I make for the Hoe, where Abigail links her arm in mine, and we seek the shade of the east tower. For once, Abigail holds her tongue, and I'm glad to let her draw me back to a world that I know.

Hester says I cannot hide away.

She squeezes my hand and walks me down to the waterside. Cool mists cover the horizon, and the wind already warns of the cold days to come. Small boats, sailing in on the high water, throw out their stinking catch. Seagulls scavenge for fish heads in the scummy water.

Everybody greets Hester and smiles at me, even the men hauling in their fishing nets, naked from the waist up, their skins as brown as mine. Some of them are smoking clay pipes. I jump at every sound: coalmen and carters and barrels rumbling over the cobbles. I am saddened to see horses staggering under the weight of so many sacks.

By the steps to the water, men and women shout out their goods: candles, meat, cheese, fish and thin strips of brightly colored cloth – all the colors of the rainbow – and I think of my friend, Amitola, born on a day of rain and rainbow and named for it. Hester sees the longing in my eyes, and she lets me choose some, softer than the hare's ear I stroked as a child.

On the way back to Whimple Street, we turn into a dismal lane, one of many, passing through streets so narrow that the roofs almost touch above the filthy water that runs between them. One lane widens and it would have been sun-filled, except for the thick smoke belching from the chimney of a wooden house.

As the smoke thins, I see a horse – a stallion – tied to a ring on the wall, pawing the ground with its left hoof, raising dust. It is the color of honey with patches the color of my skin.

I hear my mother's words: *I do not understand, Nadie. But if the gods have given you this, time will tell us why.*

When the young men of my village went into the wilderness to seek the spirit who would guide them through their lives, they would come back with tales of their visions: a wide-winged eagle, a fleet-footed lion, a strong bear. Only Seekanauk never told us of his vision quest, but we gave him that name anyway, for the crayfish that scuttles as he does, the only one of my village not to walk straight and tall. I wanted to seek a vision, too, but it was not the custom for our women.

I went anyway, last winter, when I was fourteen summers old, when my father was away hunting. Faint from lack of food, I squatted under a silver birch tree by the great lake and asked my guiding spirit to show itself. I waited for hours, shivering, watching for a great bird or a shooting star, listening for a wolf call or a growling bear, until in my mind I saw a creature pawing the ground in front of me, a creature the pale men call a horse.

I did not wonder, as my mother did, although there were few horses in our land. I had my own guiding spirit at last – and that was enough for me.

Now I put out my hand.

"What are you doing?" An older woman is standing in the doorway, fanning herself. She is no taller than me, but plump, unsteady on her feet. "So *thee's* the little Indian maid," she says. Anger silences me. "Well, has cat got thy tongue?" And the thought of those spitting, spiteful creatures I have seen in the streets of Plymouth makes me shiver. When she sees Hester, the woman sinks to the ground with her greeting, and invites us inside.

As soon as we enter the doorway, a great heat forces the breath from my body. Flames leap in the chimney around a lump of flesh hanging over the fire. It is roasting and spitting out sparks. Tom is walking through the smoke toward me, his face blackened and beaded with sweat. The tip of the stick he carries glows redder than the fire.

...flames light the length of my mother's body and lick around her slender neck...above her, leaves shrivel and branches blacken...pale men, their armor glinting, swing their fire torches against the early sunrise...

Hester, the woman, Tom: they have all tricked me. They are all my enemies. *Popogusso.* With their soothing sighs and honeyed words, they have brought me to the pit of hell.

The ribbons flutter from my hands, and I fall with them.

Tom

I didn't mean to frighten her again. The fire was safe in my hands, although she didn't know it. We lift Nadie and sit her on my stool, away from the fire.

"Her name's Nadie," my mother says.

"I *know,* mother. *Everybody* in Plymouth does."

"I am better." Nadie's voice is strong, but her eyes still glance at the chimney.

"It's a pig's heart," I say. "We hang it there to stop evil spirits coming down the chimney at night."

Mistress Hester wants to take her home. But she asks to stay. We let her watch as I shoe the stallion. He's usually a difficult horse. He belongs to the Mayor of Plymouth, who bought him because he was spirited and ran fast. But his stable boy discovered the old trick – a hedgehog had been tied under its tail.

"Come and stroke him when you're calm," I tell her. "Horses can hear your heartbeat. If you're afraid, they think there's danger close by and they stay away."

Nadie, breathing deeply, pats the horse's flanks. He swings his face toward her, drawing back his lips and putting out his tongue. When she strokes his nose, he arches his neck and licks her face.

Then Nadie laughs, and I smile at the sound. I rip off the worn-out horseshoe, clean his hoof and measure the new one. Then I heat it in the fire and feel the rush of the race to shape it. As soon as it's cooled in the barrel of water, I hammer it home. Nadie flinches at the first nail, until I explain that hoofs, like our nails, are dead.

I'm aware of her eyes on me. And my mother's, too,

for she rarely watches me work. It reminds her too much of my father.

When I finish, Nadie claps. And that's the moment the fire enters my heart.

Hester does not know what to do with me. I am neither fish nor fowl, and I disturb the order of their life in the vicarage. I have never known a young woman like Hester. She does not work in the fields. She does little work in the house. And she has no children. I ask her why.

"Ah!" She smiles. "I am Henry's sister, not his wife. As you can see, I try to keep the world away so that he can concentrate on God. God comes first. Then his sheep. That is what he calls the people who come to the church." She bites her lip. "Then me, although I suppose that I am one of his sheep. My brother is spare with his words, except in the pulpit. Then he is a different man, fired with love for God."

"But do you not want to marry? You are too young to choose such a life."

Hester blushes. "No, I do not think so. I do not know."

"A Secotan woman is pitied if she does not have children. She will marry a man she does not love to have them."

"I am happy to care for my brother. We are part of God's family, and that is enough for us."

I have never imagined such a life: no marriage, no children. But I suppose that, like me, Hester has never been in love.

As the days passed, I could not forget the magic in the forge, where the metal changed shape under the fire. But I forgot my fear. I forgot about the flames crackling behind me. I thought only about the horse – and Tom.

Hester agrees that I can go out alone to buy the bread. She sees the restlessness in me, for I am used to being outside. It is the most difficult thing I have ever done, walking through Saint Andrew's Cross, where the butchers are cutting up their meat and throwing their scraps into the water channel that runs straight to the sea.

The baker's shop is at the front of a wooden house, in the lane next to Whimple Street. The front door has been cut in half, like a stable door. The top is tied back. Underneath, stands a table, full of loaves.

How my mother would have loved it. She hated the hours she had to spend pounding corn into flour.

A girl with pale skin and hair pushes a loaf toward me. There are other loaves, smaller and scented, and straight from the oven.

Curious, I ask, "What are they?"

"Tiddy oggies." Her face is sour and as sharp as a rat's.

"I – I do not understand."

"Tiddy oggies." Her fingers tap the table.

"Give me one, please." She points to my purse and confusion fills me. Hester only lets me carry the pennies for our loaf, for fear of cutpurses. "I did not think... forgive me." Hester has taught me to say this whenever I am not sure of myself.

The girl sniggers. "*Forgive me,*" she mimics. She looks me up and down. "Pa says only people who work in the fields have brown skins. He says your kind was born white, but you've roasted in the sun."

I do not know what to say to her. I drop my coins onto the table. I go back the way I walked with Hester, the way that takes me past the forge. Then the fire frightened me. Now it draws me in.

Tom is alone.

"What are tiddy oggies?" I snap.

"Pasties." He sees my furious face. "Don't mind Abigail." He pats the flanks of a gray horse. "She's as difficult as this one. Now...just touch her right leg, at the knee."

The horse stands still for me, as it does for Tom. I touch its leg, and it lifts its hoof. I forget Abigail.

Tom's voice cuts across my thoughts. He speaks

slowly, like most of the people in Plymouth. My tongue is like the sound of a young deer pattering through the forest, young and playful, whilst the tongue of the people here is like a deer at the end of the chase, gasping and half-dead. "Are there really bears as big as the church spire in your land?" he asks. "An' snakes that wind around your body and squeeze the breath out o' you? My friend Josiah says there are sea creatures that'll sink a ship."

"I – I have seen none of these things. We just fish and grow corn and collect berries. Just as I have seen your people do."

"So you don't pack up your houses and carry them away?"

"NO! We are not turtles, Tom. We live in wooden houses with streets and gardens and fields. But it *is* different. The colors are brighter. The birds are noisier. And it is cleaner."

I want to tell him about the Mangoak, and how the shadow of that tree hung over my childhood, but I do not want to spoil the moment.

❊ ❊ ❊

"Why do you not like me?" I have asked Abigail the question many times in my head whenever I went to buy bread, but the hostility on her face always stopped me. But today, I say the words aloud and I am pleased with myself.

"What?" Her voice cracks like a crab's claw. She leans across the table and takes hold of my ear, twisting it hard. "Tom whispers things when we're alone together...things you don't even know the word for. He's *mine*!"

I slap her hand away. "We cannot own people or things," I say. "My people share everything..." I have put it badly, for Abigail crows.

"Even your men and women? Huh, that's ungodly!"

She turns her back and begins to knead the dough with the fury of a woman possessed by evil spirits.

And once more, I ask myself another question. How am I going to survive in a land where even the horses wear silver shoes? Where I have to watch everything I do and everything I say?

Tom

I know by the way my mother clenches her lips that Nadie isn't welcome at the forge. Oh, she fusses over her, says how pretty her hair is now that her fringe has grown out. But she never touches her. She sits on the stool by the chimney, for it's cold now with the door open, sipping ale, her cheeks flushed, her eyes half-closed. She talks about Francis, how *he* should have been working the forge, wondering why he left us to be a schoolmaster in Tavistock.

I hate the days when she's here.

Yesterday, she slipped from the stool, and lay laughing with her legs in the air, like a pig on its back. Nadie helped her to her feet, patted her face, but my mother stared at her hand until she removed it. Then she straightened her cap and went into the house.

"She grieves for your father," Nadie says.

"Aye, everybody calls her the Widow now. And she grieves for Francis. She doesn't drink when he's here."

"You are lucky to have a brother. I am an only child, which is unusual in my people. It is a sign of my father's great love for my mother that he did not take another wife to give him the son he wanted."

"Abigail says that your people—"

Her eyes flash. "I do not want to hear what Abigail says. Is it true that you whisper words I do not know when you are alone?"

"Abigail lets her tongue run away with her. It's true, I once thought... I was lonely after my father died, and Francis left. But she's not for me."

And I bite my lip.

I can't afford to pay a boy to puff the bellows,

and Nadie's glad to do this for me. I teach her how to heat the metal, how to hammer it into a horseshoe, and how to nail on a horseshoe. She likes the way the metal glows like sunset, curves under the hammer, hisses in the cold water.

"Why does Master Henry not keep horses in his stables?" she asks.

"He did, until last year. He rode a white mare...the gentlest I'd ever worked with. She fell into the bog up on Dartmoor. Struggled so much, she sank in seconds. If she'd stayed quiet, she might not have gone under. They might have got her out."

Nadie's eyes fill with tears. "I – I did not think it was possible to love a creature that was not human," she whispers. "I have often sat in the sun by the creek and watched the frogs jumping in the reeds, marveled at their colors, laughed at their croaking. But I have never loved a frog. We only roast them over the fire."

This land is slowly revealing its magic to me, for Hester is teaching me to read.

Last week, she showed me a book, but the shapes that she called letters meant no more to me than insects scuttling across a vine leaf. We do not have written words in my tongue. Then she gave me a book with pictures, although I could not find sunflowers, squash or corn. She pointed to a picture of a house and wrote five shapes underneath: *house*. Then a picture of a horse, like the one I had seen in my vision. When I saw that one of the letters underneath was different, understanding flashed through me.

Now I am learning to read with the hunger of somebody who has been starved. I read until my eyes water, until my candle burns out. And I can feel my fingers itching to write the letters myself. It is only when I begin to read that I no longer think in my tongue. I miss the sound of it in my head, its clicks and rhythms.

"Think of what you might learn if you stayed with us," Hester says. "You will forget what we have taught you when you are working in the fields."

My sharp voice scolds her. "That is much more use to my people," I say. But in my heart, I agree with her.

"Forgive me," she replies.

Although the days now bring me Tom, I am a creature of the night. I am happier in the dark – the color of my skin – away from the constant clamor of the daylight, the constant gawping.

It has not taken me long to learn how much Tom's

people dread nightfall. As soon as the darkness deepens, the serving-girl carries out the shutting-in. Doors are bolted and barred, windows closed, candles lit at the first shadows. She laughs when I ask if it is to keep away evil spirits.

"No, no! Only simple souls believe that. It is because the dark brings fevers and colds, not evil."

I often pull back the bolt of the kitchen door and slip outside, as silent as a spirit. I keep away from the waterside, having come to know what *whore* means. I keep away from Saint Andrew's Cross, with its beggars sleeping along its walls. I am content to make a short walk up and down Back Lane.

It is magical, especially on starry nights. There is little to disturb my stargazing, except the sheep or a beggar in the hedgerow cursing as I creep by. Only the rain stops me, for then clouds hide the moon too much.

In Secota, the leaves linger for a long time, until they crisp. Here, they lie rotting in damp mists which come with the darkness. The hedgerows smell of decay from unpicked blackberries. Some nights, caught between the moor and the sea, the fog never lifts. The wind comes from the west, coming from my people, and I listen for their voices in the wind.

Did Hester know? Sometimes she glances at my muddy shoes, the hem of my dress. But she never asks. She knows that I am a restless spirit.

From what I observe in this land, the moon and sun rise and fall, the stars pattern the sky, the Thunderbirds bring storms and its people pray to their spirits to look after them as we do. These thoughts calm me and help me to forget the flames that lit my mother's body. I feel the change in me. I am more settled in my mind. Although I still feel her loss every day, now I see her in my mind as I loved her: squatting by her pots, tongue hanging, her painting stick dipped in color, refusing to use the bristle stick that Master White offered her.

I am pleased with myself. I am making the best of what the gods have given me until I go home, for if Master White keeps his promise, I shall see my father again and honor my mother's grave.

Tom

A catchy wind blows me to Old Josiah's forge. It's on the east side of Plymouth and better placed for the London road – except that he and Josiah shoe few horses. They're skilled in making blades, sickles and scythes. *They* don't mend old women's cooking pots. *They* don't sharpen their knives for nothing.

But my feet drag in spite of the wind, for I'm envious of my friend and his father, although I've been looking forward to this all year: our rehearsal for the Saint

Clement's celebration. He's the patron saint of blacksmiths, and we remember his day at the end of November, when the moon's full. From harvest, we smiths talk of little else.

I hurl a stone into the sea. *Everything's* changed. Only a prentice can be chosen to light the gunpowder on the anvil, and I'm no longer one. They can't bend the rules for me.

Josiah's is a fine forge – built of stone, with a wide chimney that could hang a whole pig, and the best anvil in Plymouth, that gives a clear, high-pitched ring. The tools that hang on the wall are shining and well oiled. But I keep telling myself: tools are only as good as the craftsman who works them.

Night frosts are already pinching, and the fire's stoked high. There's more than twenty of us, supping ale, scoffing tiddy oggies as we gossip.

Old Josiah sucks his pipe as he waits. "Thee's as full of soot as that chimney," his wife scolds. He's not yet forty, but we call him old because he's Josiah's father. He bangs his hammer for silence.

"I know what thee's gossiping about, lads…that

young maid from beyond...some of ye more than the rest...but let's get to the task in hand."

He's right. Although I say little about Nadie, I can see her in the flames. She's walking past me, skin like burnished metal, the copper dangling at her ears, eyes fixed and wide like those of a crazed horse. There's no trace of Abigail in that fire. I can't bear to watch the prentice when he lights the gunpowder. But I see Nadie in the trail of red sparks that rise from it.

Then we circle the fire, sing in the light of the forge and talk of the Spanish armada that might sail to our shores, of the Queen who's commanded fire beacons to be placed along the coast, to be lit if England's invaded. And we place bets on who'll be chosen to make the beacon for Plymouth Hoe.

I've been watching for Nadie all morning, wondering if the cold will keep her away. But she flings open the door, puts down her bread basket and, seeing my mother isn't there, sets to work. But her hands, numb with cold, can't hold the hammer. She warms them by the fire.

"This is nothing, Tom! The cold in my land can freeze your fingers off."

When I plunge the hot iron into the water, our faces glisten in the rising steam, our hands sweat until the horse shifts, snorting with impatience and we let go.

Her skin gleams like polished metal. Her eyes are as bright as the fire. Her lilting voice makes my heart jump.

I want to tell her about last night in Josiah's forge. I want to kiss her.

But she's full of her new learning. "Hester says that books are our history and that people read them to try to change the world. Henry treats them as if they are holy – I must not dirty the paper, I must not turn down the corner, I must not spill milk on them..."

My face burns. I don't have such knowledge. I can write my name and follow the prayer book, but no more.

"Nay, paper perishes like we do – or burns," I scoff. "Our Queen's worked for thirty years to change England. When the paper's crumbled, when her—"

"*Her?* Your chief is a woman?"

"Aye. We have been ruled by queens for thirty-three years. When her body's just a pile of bones, this'll still be here." I pick up a horseshoe. "It'll be rusty around the edges, but somebody will dig it up in a hundred years."

Is she leaving me behind with all her learning? How long will it be before she learns that it's the fire that works the magic – not me?

Pies are making me plump again: pies with fish, pies with minced meat; pippin pies with apples, sugar and cinnamon. Pies called pasties with meat and vegetables, to wrap in a cloth and carry to the men working in the fields. Milk sweetened with honey, milk made into cream, milk made into cheesecakes.

Now I look less like my mother, for her body is slender and supple, although she bore me when she was little more than my age. Her deerskin was never the softest, her embroidery never the straightest, for she disliked such work, but her eyes were beautiful, her cheeks high-boned and gleaming, in spite of the paint that often splattered them. Then I rubbed them clean before my father came home.

Whenever my throat tightens with grief, I think of Tom. I am comfortable with him because his skin matches mine, because his skin smells of woodsmoke. He is as strong as any Secotan. But I am fearful of the change in me. When we said our prayers before breakfast, I always prayed to go home, but now I pray to see Tom.

Can a broken heart still feel love? Yes. Fire leaps inside me when I see him, warming my body and face. What better way to heal, my mother would have said. A heart is for love. If it breaks, mend it. Otherwise it will shrivel like the pig's heart in the chimney.

Hungry for my land, far from my own people, I am falling in love. But do I want to fall in love with a pale man? His people killed my mother. I *cannot* stay here. I must go back to my father and honor my mother's grave.

* * *

I am late for dinner, but Master Henry does not glance at the clock when I come in and, for once, we do not eat in silence.

"The Spanish have plundered gold from the New World," Henry sighs. "Now they want to plunder ours."

I speak, although my mouth is full. All the rules are being broken today. "Like your people want to plunder my land, sir?"

"Do not say 'my land'. It is called Virginia."

"Why?"

His face flushes. "It is named after our Queen, Nadie. She is known as the Virgin Queen. That is...a woman who has never...who is not married."

"Ah, *keegsquaw*! So my passionate land is named after a woman who has never felt passion!"

We eat in silence after that.

Henry and Hester never speak of Tom or the Widow or Abigail. There are so many things I do not understand: why Tom cannot drink wine with Henry, except in the church; why, if Abigail brings our bread, she must not knock at the front door.

I cut short my walk that night, for rain clouds are hiding the moon. I wish I could warm myself in the forge. I do not see the shadows at the corner of Whimple Street. They come at me from the dark, like evil *manitous*, cackling spirits that can take on human shape, that come to steal souls.

Panic shoots through me. Then I see that one of them is Abigail. I call out my greeting and hurry toward the vicarage, but she sends me sprawling onto the cobbles. I look at her. If I had to paint her, I would give her the face of a rat, with her sharp teeth and peering eyes. I try to get up, but, at a nod from her, the ones with her hold me down. They are young girls, their breath foul with fish and onions. Abigail flashes a knife. I close my eyes then, and wait. I have always known it, ever since they brought me to this island.

They brought me here as a sacrifice.

Then let me die with honor. I thrust my throat forward so that the cut will be quick. But Abigail bends over and releases my hair from my cap and hacks at it until I feel the evening chill on my neck. They let me stand and my knees tremble with relief.

I do not care about my hair. My cap and collar will soon hide it. I want to ask her for her knife and cut the part of my hair that really matters, to give me back the fringe that will make me look like my women.

At least they have not cut out my tongue.

Abigail speaks at last. "Tom's *mine*! Did you forget, eh?" The other girls grip my neck and pain shoots through my ears. Abigail has ripped out my earrings. She dangles them in front of me where the moonlight catches them.

I spring, soundless, like a lion taking its prey at last. They freeze as I shout, "*Melden...mutaquesunnauk... mangummenauk...melden...muta...*" My feet stamp to the rhythm of my voice and they shrink away. I take blood from my ear lobes and smear my face and fingers, moving toward them, repeating the words, laughing at them inside my head. What would they do if they knew that I was calling out *spinach*, *prickly pear* and *acorn*?

The young one screams first, and Abigail slaps her. I chant until I hear the copper clink at my feet, until

I hear them run away. But not before they have spat on me.

Satisfaction fills me as I let myself into the kitchen, as I warm myself by the kitchen fire. I know, by the look on their faces, that they will not bother me again. There will be no need to tell Hester – or Tom.

I put the earrings away with my deerskin skirt and my moccasins. They are too dangerous to wear in this land.

Hester weeps when she sees the sore skin at my ears. "Why did you not ask me, Nadie? I could have helped to remove your earrings."

"Forgive me, Hester," I murmur.

Master Henry is always talkative after Sunday church. That is when he notices me the most.

"What do you feel when you pray with us, Nadie?" he asks.

I shrug.

"Happy?"

"No, but less sad. I feel closer to my mother."

"She has gone back to the God who made her, to the person who created the first man and woman on this earth."

"The Great Spirit?"

"We call him God."

"Our great god has created smaller gods in the shape of the moon, the stars, the sun, the trees and flowers, water and every creature who lives on the earth," I mumble.

"Speak up! *We* have only one God, and he is our help in trouble."

"Our gods help us in the hunt and the harvest, as long as we please them and thank them, sir."

Henry does not reply, but opens the big book, like the one that always lies across the eagle's back. "These are God's words, written down. We all need God to reach the holy and the heavenly. We cannot reach him with the workings of our own mind, however clever we are." He fixes his eyes on me. "Would you like to belong to God's family, Nadie?"

"I have my own family on my own island, sir."

"Yes, but we all belong to another family and God

is our father. You will feel happy if you belong to it. You will feel as if a light is shining within you. And once it is there, it will never leave you."

"Like starlight or sunlight?"

"Yes, like the sun warming you all the time. That is what God's love is like. And it means you can go to Heaven when you die."

I do not know what to say.

Master Henry touches my shoulder lightly. "You could be baptized Elizabeth."

I hold myself straight and proud. Then I shake my head, slowly. "No, thank you. My name is Nadie."

Hester smiles. But her brother sighs. "You will not go to Heaven, then."

And, as the weeks pass, I feel his disappointment.

In her gentle way, as if she is aware of the change in me, Hester reminds me that I shall be going home. She lets me read the letters sent by Master White. He has met Sir Walter Raleigh in London, who has persuaded the Queen that a new colony should be established in

Virginia in the spring. Master White writes that *he* might be the Governor. He speaks of how he will soon be able to put right the terrible wrong that has been done to me. He will take me back where I belong. *Only one thing can stop me now,* he writes, *and that is a Spanish invasion.*

Planting time. A few moons at the most. I shiver. Lately, I have thought of little else but Tom – not of the past, not of the future. We have never spoken of my leaving. The dark is too precious for that.

"Are you not pleased?" Hester asks.

I should be shouting for joy, for Master White has kept his promise. Secota flashes into my mind: fields bright with sunflowers and corn, my father happy that I am alive. But Tom's face blots it out. So many emotions that my head is bursting, and Hester mistakes my tears for happiness.

Now I realize that the journey I made across the great salt water is greater than I ever imagined.

Tom

Fear hangs over Plymouth, like the black smoke that billows from every forge within its walls. It comes on the winter wind, blowing into every crack and corner, gathering strength, threatening to smash the city walls as swiftly as any Spanish cannonball. And with it come the whispers of torture and burning if we refuse to turn back to the old faith once we're conquered.

We smiths are busier than we've ever been, and the heat of our fires warms the November chill. We hammer hard, for we hate the Spanish more than we hate the devil, for their King calls our Queen a whore.

From the pulpit, the Reverend says that God will defend us. But I'm happier being defended by the fortresses that King Henry had built along the south coast, by our castle on the Hoe, by our navy.

Nor does Plymouth sleep well. Great ships are being built: the *Hope,* the *Nonpareil* and the *Revenge,* so urgently that the men work at night under flaming torches.

Old Josiah has been chosen to forge the Plymouth beacon, to be lit along with those that stretch to London and Cornwall, when the Spanish ships are sighted at sea. I curse my father again for dying. I hoped for the honor of making that beacon with him. But when the armor's brought out from the church crypt for inspection, I'm given the job of repairing and replacing the rivets that have rusted. I'm pleased with this task. In my own small way, I'm helping to defend my country.

Our daily life is geared to the threat of invasion: the daily muster of men on the Hoe for training in case the call to arms comes, the greasing of cannons, the checking of the rings that hold the chains across the harbor.

Sir Francis Drake rides down from Dartmoor. The cannons are ready. Soldiers keep watch from the towers, shouting at every cloud on the horizon.

Aye, we're all fired up for war. But while the others clamor to get even with our enemy, I harbor a secret thought: I want war so that Master White can't sail to Virginia, so that he can't take Nadie from me.

"Master Henry thinks the Spanish people should be satisfied with what they have," Nadie says. "He's right. Men cannot own land. They cannot own trees and soil and animals and birds, any more than they can own the sun and the moon and the stars. We must share them all."

"Tell that to Sir Francis and Sir Walter," I say.

My mother hisses her anger. We didn't hear her come into the forge. "Don't scoff, son. Sir Francis has done more for Plymouth than anybody I know. He's paying for water to be piped from his own pocket."

"From the river, surely, mother?"

She scowls. "He's given more to the church than any other man."

"That's because he's wealthy. He owns half the houses in Plymouth."

"Sir Francis is very devout. He spends hours in prayer—"

"They say he will attack the Spanish in their own country, before they can attack us here," Nadie interrupts. "How much gold and silver will he take this time?"

My mother shrieks. "How dare *thee* – a stranger! – come to our land and mock him?"

"I have heard the seamen say that he has special magic powers to move around the world," Nadie goes on. I frown my warning. "We have such men. They can travel at night—"

My mother moves with the speed of lightning. She's too quick for me, for I've got to make the hot metal safe. She pulls Nadie over to the barrel and pushes her face into the water. "*Magic powers?* Don't use thy evil tongue against Sir Francis. Wash out thy foul and filthy mouth!"

I try to take Nadie from her, but she's strong with drink and dislike. She pulls Nadie's dress from her shoulder and rubs at her tattoo. "*We're* made in God's image. Decorating our bodies is devil's work."

Nadie struggles free. She shakes her hair, showering my mother with water. Most girls I know would look ugly with their hair bedraggled, their faces wet. But Nadie's skin glistens, and her hair – shorter than I remember – curls wild around the nape of her neck.

She's beautiful.

"*We* believe that tattoos are the only way our people will recognize us in death," she says. "Otherwise, we wander the spirit world. They are all we take with us to the next world."

"*Spirits! Magic powers!* I've had enough of your nonsense." My mother pushes Nadie out of the door. "Now get out o' my sight and keep out o' it!" she shouts.

I go after her. Oh, Nadie. Sometimes it's better to keep your tongue still.

The days are as dark as the nights. I do not let myself think of Tom. I turn my back to the fire in the parlor, so that I cannot see his face in the flames. As the days shorten, the rain hardens white and stings my skin.

I live next to the dead in the burying ground. I see how the pale people grieve for the ones they have lost, placing flowers on the green mounds. But Tom does not come to his father's grave.

I think that love is like a corn seed in the ground.

If there is rain to nourish it, it grows under the ground until it pushes its way through to the light. I hope that by not feeding my love, it will die.

But my spirits are low and, pleading sickness, I do not go out, even to buy bread. I want to tell Hester. I have wanted to tell her about Tom for a long time, but I was afraid that she would forbid me to see him. But now I have brought that about with my own tongue.

Then, like a wild turkey tempted by a trail of acorns, Plymouth forces me outside: the pedlar with his rainbow ribbons, the sugared plums, pins and lace and gloves. I crave them all, and Hester indulges me, for they lure me outside.

On my way back, I pass Tom in Saint Andrew's Cross. We touch hands briefly.

"If I do not wash after work, nobody will see us in the dark," he whispers. "At nightfall, man and bush look alike."

"And so do dogs and wolves."

I cannot stay away from him. We become creatures of the night. The days keep Tom from me, but the darkness of the lane gives him back to me. We stand next to shimmering spiders' webs, grass glinting in the full-moon frost; silent except for the swish of my skirts as he pulls me closer so that I can flutter my eyelashes against his cheek. And the night, which most people fear, is our friend.

You could see me in the dark if my skin was white, I think.

When I let him kiss me for the first time, I know that is what he wants by the way he presses his body against me, so hard that I stagger and he curves his arm around my waist to hold me up. And the fire inside me burns as brightly as ever.

The great beacon is ready. It stands on the Hoe, filled with wood and ready to light. But the winter storms come early, spilling their waves over the harbor wall, and the Spanish are forgotten. They will not sail until spring.

Master Henry has told me about Mary, who gave birth to Jesus although she was a *keegsquaw,* and I wonder, too, if I will give birth to the Son of God, for I've grown fatter every day.

But in these dark days, my woman's blood comes back to me and Hester, thinking it is my first time, takes great pains to explain it to me. I let her. But I cannot tell her how much I miss bathing in the river at such times, how ashamed I feel that the kitchen girl has to wash my bloody cloths and dry them over the fire.

Tom

Crowds have been gathering since dusk at the Cross, for the Saint Clement's Day celebrations. Josiah and I light the fire baskets on the wall. The polished metal of the anvil gleams, as do the faces of the smiths of Plymouth circled around it. The fire's been burning since noon. I grip the handle of the bellows so tightly that my knuckles whiten, and flames leap into the spitting rain.

The prentice takes his place by the anvil.

I wish it was *my* anvil. I wish my father was here to see *me* light the gunpowder.

I search the crowds for sight of Nadie. She turns in from Whimple Street, just in time to hear the Reverend's short prayer. Then he nods at Old Josiah, the builder of beacons, who shouts for silence. "You've all heard of King Alfred," he roars. "Well, one day, he was stupid enough to say that his *tailor* was the best of all his craftsmen." The crowd hisses. "So all his blacksmiths laid down their tools: hammers, tongs and pokers. They refused to work." The crowd cheers. "Soon, the carpenters couldn't do their jobs because their tools were broken. The horses couldn't work in the fields because the ploughs were broken. So the King set his own men to work the forge as best they could. But they were so clumsy that..."

He nods. The prentice pulls a rod from the fire and lights the gunpowder. An explosion shatters the air. Smoke belches. "...they overturned the anvil with a loud bang."

A grotesque figure wobbles on stilts through the rising smoke. "I am Saint Clement," he hisses through his beard, "and I have come to restore order – and teach the King of England a lesson." He turns to face us, pointing with a long finger. "Learn a lesson from this sorry tale. Our carpenters need nails, saws and hammers. The stonemasons need mallets and chisels. The carters need axles and our shipbuilders need nails and fittings." He points to the circle of smiths. "Our craftsmen depend on the blacksmith. But the blacksmith depends on *no* other."

Pride surges through me. I watch Nadie through the starry smoke, her face alight with happiness.

A bear was brought to town for our entertainment – an old one this year, its nose scarred, its fur ragged. We pay a penny to sit on a wooden bench. Gentlemen hold their horses still as they rear at the bear's roar. Fruit sellers pester us to buy apples, pears and nuts.

The bear, roped around the ankles to a ring in the wall, punches the air. He growls and snaps at us with his paws. He paces backward and forward, as far as his rope allows him. A boy holds up a flaming torch. Then I realize.

The bear's eye sockets are gaping holes of crusted blood.

The crowd parts, letting through five men, each holding a bulldog pulling at its chains. Bets are placed. Then, yapping, the dogs leap at the bear, snapping at its thighs. Tufts of fur float to the ground, splattering blood. One dog, bigger than the others, bites the bear's buttocks and it roars with rage and pain.

"Now they'll try to get him by the throat!" Abigail shouts.

In that moment, as Abigail stands up to see better, Nadie stands in front of the bear. The dogs rear in surprise, as their owners pull them back. People leap to their feet, calling for her to get down.

"Set the dogs on her!" The crowd takes up the chant.

My mother holds me back. "Leave the wild animals together," she says. And I stay with them. I don't know what to do. In truth, I feel as captive as the bear.

Nadie raises her arms, shouting into the crowd. "Leave this poor creature alone and feast your eyes upon *me*, the exotic flower from Virginia. We do not taunt animals in my land."

"No, you just shoot 'em with bows and arrows," the bear owner shouts.

"We kill them, it is true, but gently and with care, and we thank them for giving their lives for us. If the men of Secotan have not killed a bear by the longest night, we worry for the winter. Fur and food – they make a difference between life and death. This poor creature would feed my people for weeks."

"I'm earning an honest living," the bear owner protests, "and I've paid good money for my license. It's better than begging. If bear-baitin' be good enough for the Queen, it be good enough for us. Now stand aside, lass!"

But Nadie refuses. Like a fire that has been smoldering all night, my love for her bursts into flames that almost reach the sky. I stand up. My mother hisses, "Stay where you are, son."

One of the men holding a dog picks up a handful of dung and throws it at Nadie. But as I reach her, the crowd cheers and whistles. Not at me, not at Nadie, but at the bear that has chewed through his rope. Now he's running toward the church.

"God's saved him for now," Abigail yells. "You'll have to make a chain for him next time, Tom."

I watch the fire all night. Nadie's face dances in the flames. The pig's heart swings in the heat. It hasn't stopped evil spirits from entering our world. They've taken hold of my mother, of her mind and body. I feel a great sadness for all of us – for our broken family that cannot mend. I cut the string that holds the heart and let it drop into the fire.

And I curse Nadie for coming into my world. Now that the threat of war's over for the winter, there's talk only of Sir Walter's new colony in Virginia. Already I dread the coming year that'll take her from me.

Is it too late? I learned my first lesson of love when my father died. Love's being part of somebody else. But in parting with Nadie, I'll be giving up a part of myself again.

Outside, the sky brightens into dawn. The church clock chimes seven times. The firewood's hardly glowing.

For the first time in months, my mind's clear.

It is the tradition on the night before Christmastide for the church tower to be open, for Henry feels that people should be closer to God on the night that His son was born, and closer to the star that hung over His birthplace. And, Hester says, the collecting box at the foot of the tower will take enough money to pay for its repairs.

Glowing fires are already roasting pigs and sheep in the burying ground, and smaller ones roast chestnuts and apples stuffed with raisins, and warm wine sprinkled with spices. Tom's fire is close to the church porch, and snowflakes melt on my cheeks at the sight of him. He's almost dancing: twisting and tapping as he shapes buttons and hooks to sell, and lucky charms to ward off evil spirits now that the nights never seem to end.

Tom's brother Francis, newly arrived from Tavistock, greets me with a bow. The Widow looks away. He has her dark hair and pale skin, but not her coolness. He wants to know everything about me, and about my land. "You are Devon's most famous stranger," he says. He asks me questions that nobody else has asked, not even Tom. How do we keep our soil so fertile? How do we catch our fish? But there is an air of fragility about him, an air of innocence – like Seekanauk.

We have to wait until all the important people of Plymouth have made their climb, breathless under their heavy jewels and clothes. It is pride that makes my people important, not frills and ruffs.

At last, Henry takes us to the tower door. Francis is sitting with his mother by the collecting box, and I ask him why he is not coming with us. But Tom shakes his head at me. Hester holds my hand, and we climb behind the boy with the torch. I climb slowly, afraid that the tower will topple and hurl me to the ground, watching the sun slant through the window slits to calm me.

"Two hundred and fifty!" Tom says. "We're nearly there."

He opens a small door and we step out onto the roof. The wind softens. The sun has almost set, showing a starry sky. I have never been so close to the sky, so close to the Upper World that lies beyond. I feel close to my mother. I do not see Plymouth below us, only the moonlight lighting its path to her.

The others, grumbling as they chill, start to climb down, leaving only Tom and me. As the torch flickers from the stairway, Tom wraps his arms around my waist, kisses the back of my neck. I can feel his heartbeat against my spine.

"Don't go home," he whispers.

Words I dread to hear and words I want to hear, sweet on his tongue, melting in my ear. He turns me around and his green eyes, bright with love, look straight at me as they did that first day.

I do not know what to say. So I stay silent, happy to

know that Tom loves me. And he does not press me for a reply. We watch the moon lighting the sea that brought me here. Then we climb down, hearts beating faster, minds full of wonder at what has happened.

"Well?" the Widow asks. "Was it worth the climb?"

"Oh, yes," I tell her. "It took my breath away."

In the lane, after Christmastide, after Francis has left for Tavistock, winter bites with sharp teeth. I do not know the words of love in the English tongue for I have never needed them, and I do not recognize Henry's call to love Jesus in the feelings I have for Tom. I use my eyes instead. Then Tom looks back at me with loving eyes, and we laugh, easy with each other.

"I wish I had eyes like Hester's. They are like the sea, misty with clouds of gray."

"You're stuck with muddy brown as if the tide's gone out." He tweaks my hair. "And hair like seaweed."

"All my people are like this. But I have my father's nose and his lopsided mouth."

My heart grows hot as if a fire has entered it, and

when Tom kisses me, flames stir everywhere: in my arms and legs and belly.

"Well, will you stay?" he asks.

I shiver at the thought of going back to Secota when my mother is not there. But will people whisper behind my back and point if I stay with Tom? Abigail already thinks I have bewitched him. Could there be a life for me – for us – here?

"How can I honor my mother's grave if I stay?" I ask Tom. "I want to be a good daughter as you have been a good son. And I long to see my father. I am all he has now." I shiver. "I do not know, Tom."

"Hush..."

Then we prolong our meeting with kisses and loving caresses.

Tom

My mother's still up when I get back to the forge. She asks me if I've been with Abigail.

I don't know if she's silly with ale or not when I tell her that I love Nadie. She closes her eyes and sways. "Thee's hot-headed, Thomas, *and* a fool." Her eyes gleam suddenly. "Anyhow, thee can't marry her, not in church. She's a heathen."

I haven't thought so far. *Marry?* But her anger makes me bold. "Then we'll declare our marriage at the tavern.

Josiah and his father will witness it."

"That's not a proper marriage, not in my eyes."

"It's lawful, though."

"And where shall thee live? Not *here*. I won't have her under my roof." Her voice softens. "Thee can't see beyond her black skin, Thomas. They say it's what every man dreams of. But underneath it, she's just a simple soul. Lie with her before she leaves, Thomas, if thee must. Get it out of your blood. But don't *marry* her." She shudders. "The thought of thee being with her makes my flesh crawl."

"On my father's grave, I swear you wouldn't say that if she was Abigail. It's *not* Nadie's way to lie together before marriage, although it may have been yours." I pick up my hammer and swing it in the air. "I wish the Spanish dogs would brave the winter storms. They'd stop Master White in his tracks. And I'd kill a hundred of them with one blow from my hammer. I'd split open their skulls without a thought."

My mother moves away from me, her anxiety only lifting when the forge door opens. Abigail and Walter are standing there.

"Come an' talk some sense into this fool," she says. "He thinks he's in love with his Indian maid."

But they mock me from the doorway.

"I hear thee's got a way with horses, Tom," Walter shouts. "I hear thee's only got to touch their knees and they lift their leg." Sweat gathers on my neck. "Aye, they do what thee wants."

"Get out."

"What did your exotic fruit taste of?" Abigail taunts.

I hurl the hammer at them as they leave and it cracks the ice on the cobbles.

I wish that nobody knew. Our love is better in the darkness of the lane than brought into the daylight.

I undress in the candlelight. My tattoo used to be the envy of my friends, for my mother's skill lay in her patterns. Now it is faded.

I pull on my deerskin skirt that scarcely covers my womanhood now that I am plump. *This is the last one I shall make for you,* my mother said, *for now you are a woman and must make your own.* She did not have the patience to soften the skin as she should so that it was as smooth as a new leaf. It still puckers where the skin is too hard, like a leaf shriveling under the harvest moon.

I am almost ready. I hang bone and pearl necklaces around my neck. I dare not put back my copper earrings for the holes have scarred, dare not cut my fringe. But I coil back my hair.

Let Tom see me once more as I really am.

Tom

Snow narrows the lane and clings to the hedgerows. Fishing boats lie iced in the harbor below. We find warmth in the stables. I go to embrace Nadie, to ask her to marry me, but she pulls away from me, and I wonder if I've frightened her.

I keep my distance, waiting for her to come to me. I hear the swish of her cloak as it falls to the ground. "Look, Tom," she whispers. My breath quickens. Moonlight pours through the stable grating.

I see her as I saw her that first day, and – like that day – everything else slips away from me in that moment. "Feast your eyes as you did before. I know that you love me, but do you know with whom you have fallen in love?" She takes my hand and puts it under her breast so that I can feel her heartbeat. "*Do* you?"

Love for her grips me like the tide of the ocean, taking me backward and forward. It blots out everything: the forge, Abigail, even my mother.

It's easy to ask her to marry me. I take my hand from her heart and touch her wedding finger. "Aye, Nadie, I know who you are. And I'll make you a copper ring, I promise."

Marry. I did not understand what that meant in this island, and that was my mistake.

A flush warms Henry's face, mottling his skin scarlet like a wild turkey. His mouth opens and closes in silence, until his breathing calms. Then his words shower like sparks in the air: *disloyalty...disrespect...disregard...sin.* But his anger is quiet. He seems to shrivel.

"What have I done wrong, sir? My mother said it was the greatest gift of the gods to fall in love."

"It would be a sin against God if Thomas married you. You believe in many gods, Nadie. You are not part of God's family because you refused to be baptized. *'All those who make idols are worthless',"* he said, "'*and the gods they prize so highly are useless. Those who worship these gods are blind and ignorant, and they will be disgraced.*'"

"God. Gods. What does it matter? When I pray to my Great Spirit, I am filled with sunlight, as you are when you pray to yours."

Henry paces the parlor. "There is the shadow of sin hanging over you. No, you cannot marry *him*. It would have been better for us all if they had never brought you here. What am I going to tell John when he arrives tonight? You *shall* go home, Nadie. You *shall* go back to your own people."

"HENRY." Hester is crying.

"Baptize me then. I am ready."

For a moment, his eyes glint. Then he shakes his head. "No, NO. You can only join God's family if you want to. It is too late. I cannot do it just because you have fallen in love." He looks straight at Hester. "I hold you responsible, sister. Why did you not keep her closer to you? Why have you let her roam Plymouth like a wild animal?"

Hester does not reply, but her cheeks color. She stays with me after Henry has left the room. I wait for her soft tongue to sharpen, but it does not. And, in that way, she is as dear to me as my own mother.

"Shall you really marry him?"

"I do not know what to do, Hester. I want to go home to see my father, but now that I love Tom, I have a foot in both worlds. It is not my fault. I did not ask for this."

"Then you must put your feet together and walk soon," she replies, "for Master White comes before nightfall. I fear for you, Nadie, whether you are here or there, for the trouble it will bring you."

"Love cannot bring trouble," I protest. But my heart sinks.

"It is natural, Nadie, for you to have strong feelings for a young man. You are at that age when the past and the future hardly exist. It is an age when you can take risks..."

"Am I being unwise, Hester?" My voice is shaking.

"I do not know. I know of nobody who has chosen to

be with a person of a different skin. What color will your children be?"

Children?

There was such a child born in our village two summers ago – a baby boy so pale that people accused his mother of lying with one of the pale men. Others said the boy had an evil spirit trapped inside him, sucking the color from his eyebrows, eyelashes and hair. Everybody called him the body without a soul. He did not live long. His skin scorched and swelled in the sun and he died, screaming in agony.

Hester, seeing my distress, takes me in her arms.

"Have I done something wrong?" I ask.

"No, you have fallen in love, that is all," she replies. And her voice is wistful.

I go to the church, instead of the lane. I want to touch the stone bowl that holds the holy water, the one used to baptize the babies.

It is only a water mark on my forehead. How can it mean so much? It is a mystery to me.

God, gods. The difference is only one letter, the letter in the shape of the snake.

Can I do it? Then I can marry Tom.

The snake uncurls its tongue and hisses its warning. It is poised to sink its fangs into my skin. It sways backward and forward, fascinating me, holding my eyes until I shake my head and it shrinks back to size.

Long after the house is quiet, I stand at the window, looking out across the water. Sleet hisses in the chimney. A horse clatters in the street. I can see him from the window, cheeks glowing above his fur-trimmed cloak from the uphill ride to Whimple Street: Master White riding hard to reach Plymouth ahead of the snow, coming to recruit more colonists, and coming to paint my portrait for Hester and Henry before he takes me home.

I see the fire in Master White at last. It tells me that he already knows. His anger takes me by surprise. It is the deep anger that lies at the heart of each of us. We can hide it under small kindnesses and smiles, but it always forces itself to the surface in the end. I would have run from him if he had not turned the key in the lock.

Where is the kindly man who gave me his cabin and slept on deck in the foulest storm because of me? Like the old bear, he swipes the air with his fists, blind with rage.

"You *will* go back, Nadie. There is no question of you staying. I have worked for months for this. Wheeling and dealing with Walter Raleigh, with Hariot, with the Queen, to settle in Virginia. I shall not give it up."

"I am not asking you to give it up, sir."

"My...the colony would be under threat if you stayed. Your people would be baying for my blood if I did not take you back. *Ergo*...so...you must go with me. I am the Governor of the City of Raleigh, by the power invested in me by... By God, the Spanish shall not have *our* Virginia."

"You have lived long enough in my land to know that it is *not* yours to own, sir."

His cheeks redden briefly. Then he smashes his fist down on the table. "I have come—"

"—too far to go back?"

His voice softens like silk. "Your father will be waiting and watching for you. How he must have suffered! And a daughter who does not honor her mother's grave is worse than..."

Without another word, he sets up his easel and brushes.

"Sit by the window," he says. Confused, I do as he says. "Sunlight lightens all color, Nadie. And lightness and darkness is the most important part of painting, because I am painting on a flat surface. Yes, light and shadow will make you come alive."

He picks up a thin stick of charcoal and his hand sweeps across the parchment. "What *I* see is the most important thing, not what I think. I wish I could have kept you as you were." He sighs and picks up his pots of paint. "Look, Nadie! The brown of the speckled deer, the pink of the jumping salmon, the white of oyster shells and the yellow of corn cobs."

How skilled his tongue is! My land reassembles itself in front of me, vibrant with colors.

I want to snatch the painting from him and hurl it onto the fire and watch my face crumple and blacken.

But I am afraid to do it, and my face grows hot at the thought.

"How do you know there is anything to go back to?" I whisper. "How do you know the pale men did not burn Secota to the ground?"

Master White flinches, as if I have struck him. "They would have told me," he says.

Tom

In the tavern, I learn that Sir Walter Raleigh's provided ships to return to Virginia and that the Queen has appointed Master White as the Governor of the City of Raleigh, to be established there. He's already recruited colonists in London and Essex. Now he's come to meet the great and good of Devon, wealthy families who can afford to invest five hundred pounds for fifty acres of land, and the chance to export timber and pitch and resin.

It's not for the likes of me.

As I dampen down the fire, the door of the forge opens, letting in flurries of snow and Master White. He moves like a young man as he makes for the warmth of the fire. But, in its light, I see the face of a man who's sailed far, beaten by wind and sun and worry.

I shiver. This is the man who's promised to take Nadie home.

He towers above me, eyes watering in a weary face. "I come from the West Country, boy," he says. "Sometimes, I visit the cathedral in Bristol, because I am an artist, and I go to gaze at its fine paintings. There is an engraving on the wall of the deanery, of a woman holding a flaming heart in a pair of blacksmith's tongs..." He stops and gazes into the fire.

"She *wants* to stay with me, sir." My tongue catches my teeth.

His mouth tightens. "She does not know what she wants. And there can be no talk of Nadie staying here. She is the scar on our conscience that must be healed. And to tell you the truth, boy, she does not *want* to stay. She has told me so. She does not understand our ways, in spite of all that Henry and Hester have taught her." He pauses at my gasp. Seeing my uncertainty, he hurries on. "Oh, yes, she has been seduced by books and ribbons and pretty clothes and..." His eyes travel up and down me. "What maid would not be? But she is not thinking clearly. A daughter who does not return to her father in his time of need – who does not honor her mother's grave – is worse than the devil itself... You will blame yourself...and..." He stops.

What does he want *me* to say? Who is telling the truth?

Snow blows down the chimney, spitting on the flames. He comes closer. "If you go, she will go, Thomas. Then she will have the best of both worlds." He glances around the forge. "And so will you."

The blood rushes to my head. "I've never thought of such a thing, sir... I like the walls of Plymouth. And... how would I afford it?"

"I am in great need of more carpenters, more blacksmiths. I shall take you without payment. But I warn you now that we stop at Roanoke Island only to pick up the soldiers we left last year at Fort Lane. Then we sail on to Chesapeake Bay, a hundred miles north." The names mean nothing to me. I've never been beyond Plymouth, let alone beyond the sea. "I could not let you live in Secota. We shall need you in the colony. But remember, this is a single passage. You must live by the rules of the colony. You will be working without wages." He draws breath. "She *wants* to go back, Tom."

The forge sways in front of me.

Master White lowers his voice. "Come, Tom. Now is your chance to be a man, to be the first in your family to live in the New World." His eyes range over the forge, over the row of tools hanging on the wall. "You could do better than this."

He's spoiled the moment and he knows it, for I turn from him to finish damping down the fire. "We're decent folk who've worked hard to keep ourselves, sir. We've never had to beg or borrow – or steal." My voice trembles. Then I turn back to him, looking toward the anvil. "I'm proud of all this."

He picks up a horseshoe. "This is fine work! A shoe made without love is ragged at the edges. This is the smoothest shoe I have ever seen, by God." He leans against the wall, wiping his forehead with his sleeve. "I cannot offer you horseshoes, Tom. It will be making and mending in Virginia." He pauses again, out of breath. "But here's the reward. Master Henry told me what happened to your father. You could finish your apprenticeship out there. I have a master blacksmith sailing from Portsmouth with us. Is *that* not worth it?"

"Is Nadie not worth it?" I ask.

Master White puts out his hand. "Well, will you come with me, Master Martyn? Shall we shake on it?"

I hesitate. Can I do this for Nadie? Have I the courage to go?

"Do not wait too long, Tom. Strike while the iron's hot." He laughs at his choice of words. "She *wants* to go back," he whispers.

As I said, I'm not a steady flame. I clasp his hand.

"So the fire will go out in Plymouth?"

"Yes, sir. And be lit again in Virginia."

As I search for the words to tell my mother, I imagine her cry echoing like my hammer on the anvil. But the shock stills her, and she lets out a long sigh as if she already knows. Hopes of a good dowry, the daughter she's never had – all slip away in that moment. Then she whispers, "All my men have left me."

And the wind blows hard down the chimney, puffing smuts onto her flushed cheeks, but she doesn't wipe them away.

I wait for her to go to bed, longing to go to the lane, longing to tell Nadie.

A bitter wind blows through the stable grating.

"I pity any fishing boat that hasn't turned back to shore," Tom says, his voice quivering.

I can feel his heart racing. I touch his forehead, afraid that he has one of those sudden fevers that afflict so many people in this land. He paces up and down, his body almost bursting from his skin, his breath quickening. "I'll make shovels and spades and knives. I'll mend things. I'll work hard. That's why they failed last time.

They took too many soldiers. They need young men, and women and children."

"What are you saying?"

"Didn't he tell you?" He picks me up, spins me around, then sets me on the ground again. "We'll have the best of both worlds. My world in yours! *I* can take you home, Nadie. I never dreamed that... Master White's given me free passage. I can be a prentice again."

Shock runs through me. The ship that brought me here was pushed back constantly by the wind, and I hoped it would take me home. Then, just as suddenly, it changed direction and we surged onward. Once more, I do not know which way I am going.

I had never thought of Tom in my land. I never thought that he would choose to leave the land he loved.

I want to say: Do you not see what has happened? Master White has used you. *He* cannot go back to Virginia without me. His precious colony would not survive if my people did not see me with their own eyes. I want to ask: Do you really want to come to my land?

But I cannot bear to quench the new fire in his eyes.

Tom dislikes my silence. "I've given Master White my word, Nadie. We've shaken hands on it. Perhaps your folk don't understand what that means?"

My tongue lashes. "Do not speak to me about honor! Your people sailed in friendship and ended in killing and kidnap."

"I wasn't part of that. And besides, we'll be living further north, at a place called Chesapeake, so Master White says. How many days' walk away is that from Secota?"

"How do *I* know? A few days? What life are you offering me in my land, Tom? Town boy, sipping ale in the tavern, never hunted a bear...have you been taught to shoot arrows from boyhood?" I wish I wasn't taunting him. There is more of my father in me than I realize.

"Aye, Nadie, I have. Our Queen commands all men from the age of seven to know how to use a bow and arrow. It's still a weapon of war."

"Oh..."

He soothes me with his pattering words and caresses, until I can think of nothing but being with him, whether in Plymouth or in Secota or in the City of Raleigh. Only our world matters, whichever one it is. I catch his excitement. "I shall be a useful wife, Tom. I can plait fishing weirs and plant corn. I shall protect you. I shall be more use to you than a wife who can sew and bake."

"We could marry before we sail, Nadie. We can declare it with two witnesses."

"NO. Now that you are coming to my land, I want to take you to my father."

Tom moves away from me, angry again. "How do I know that you'll marry me, once we're in Virginia?"

"We have promised each other, that is enough. Love is an invisible chain that will link us forever."

"*We* never made chains at the forge," he says. "My father hated them."

I watch Master White leave at dawn, disappearing into a woodsmoke so thick that I hardly see him ride through the town gates. A bitter wind still blows snow against the window.

He has done his job well.

Tom

I'm making nails and knives to take with me – and a small horseshoe to hang over the door of our house. I've too much time, for my customers are beginning to take their horses elsewhere. Not from spite, but because they've got to accustom their horses to new hands.

They're hard days.

Fresh wood fills the beacons, for the King of Spain's fleet is said to be ready. Everybody knows, although he thinks it's a secret. But what do I understand about the squabble of kings and queens?

The white blossom of the blackthorn shows at last against its leafless branches. Josiah, still my faithful friend, walks me to the quayside tavern, away from my mother's scolding, for she complains that the forge is dirty and the tools tarnished. A line of ships shows on the horizon, sailing from the direction of Portsmouth and London. I try to count them as they rise on the swell and then disappear. There are more than twenty. Sweat pours from me. Josiah steadies me, although his hand's trembling, too. Whilst I think it's Master White come too early, he fears it's the armada and wants to run for his father to light the beacon. But the seamen laugh and tell us they're Drake's ships, sailing to Spain, to teach the King a lesson he'll never forget.

And part of me is sorry. I wish they were Spanish ships. Then I'd not have to brave that cruel ocean. I'm ashamed, for only a coward has such thoughts.

Plymouth fills with strangers. Some are to sail with us. Some have come to say goodbye. They cluster on the quayside and stare out to sea, half-hopeful, half-afraid.

A small group of colonists will sail from Plymouth. William Lucas, a carpenter – tall and lanky with red-gold hair – his wife Mary and their son, Joshua, both small and dark-haired; Mary's sister, Agnes. All recruited in north Devon. Henry and Rose Chapman, John and Joyce Payne, farmers from Devon; Jack and Edward, twin brothers from Cornwall, and other families and their children, whose names I don't know.

Now I'm as excitable as a young bird about to take its first flight. I go to the quayside every evening to watch the boxes and chests being brought down. Most will have been loaded in Portsmouth, but Master White has ordered an extra anvil, a spare anchor, axes, picks, spades, nails and hammers. And barrels of dried beef, pork and fish, cheese, butter, rice and raisins, salt and vinegar and oil, honey, sea biscuits, apples and ale.

I try not to look beyond the quay – beyond the edge of my world.

Lanterns and candles, fishing nets, twine, hooks, nails have almost filled my box. Francis comes to say his farewell and to take our mother back to Tavistock.

He watches as I shoe the last horse. Then he takes me to the tavern, where Old Josiah pushes his pipe between my teeth.

"Better get used to it, lad. Imagine all those fields of baccy. Think on us here, scraping our pennies together to buy it."

It makes me light-headed and warms my belly. Then I cough until my eyes stream and I hand it back to him. I watch their faces in the glow of the tavern fire – my friends, my family.

"Make sure your pa-in-law don't boil you in a pot," Josiah says. "An' watch out for them snakes that wind themselves around you and squeeze the life out of you."

"You're a brave lad," his father says. "We're proud of thee, Tom, going off to a strange land like that. You're your pa's son, all right."

And his words bring on the tears, for now I'll never carry on the forge for him. I'll never see Plymouth again. I look at Francis, sitting beside me. He's loosened his collar. Ale flushes his face. "You did me a favor that day, Tom." He slips his crooked arm around my shoulders, laughs at the shock on my face. "There is no blame, brother. You were only eight."

Francis was afraid of heights from the very first time we climbed the church tower on Christmastide Eve. He trembled. Then he was sick. From then on, he waited for us at the foot of the steps. When we played our war games on the Hoe, Francis stayed close to me. Walter and Josiah didn't notice that he never climbed the towers. One day, I pushed him away, irritated. I told Walter to choose him for his army and take him up the tower. Francis was on the verge of tears, but he tried not to lose face. He disappeared into the dark doorway. A few minutes later, he gave a loud scream and tumbled down the steps.

His right arm had snapped. My father tied it to a wooden stick, but it healed badly.

"There'll be no smithing for you, son," he said.

I never told Francis what I'd said to Walter that day. He seemed pleased with his change of fortune. He stayed at school, learned his letters and came home with books that made my eyes hurt. And, when I was ten years old, my father took me on as his prentice.

But somebody whispered to my mother, because she said she'd never forgive me. Francis was the apple of her eye, and I'd bruised her precious fruit.

As we leave the tavern, I try not to look at the sea. It seems to stretch on forever.

Francis and I sit by the fire until the last flame dies out. I touch the anvil that's served me so well, now to be sold. I wrap the tools, all except the hammer, in my blanket and place them in my box. I pick up the last nails and start to hammer down the lid.

Only then do I realize: I can't pack my hammer. Then we laugh until the tears come – and we're brothers again.

I do not go far. I fear the people of Plymouth, for I am taking Tom from them. I am like the lepers that Hester has told me about. My skin is my bell.

Only the ribbon man still tempts me to show my face. I want to buy ribbons for Amitola. But Abigail and the Widow turn in from New Street. They see me before I can disappear.

Abigail sniffs the air around us. "I can smell magic potions, Mistress Martyn...love potions that you put onto men's eyes to make them fall in love."

"Abigail!" The Widow's face is scarlet. "Be silent, girl." She sees the tears in my eyes. "There's nothing stronger than first love. It holds you in its grip like ice," she whispers. "But ice gives up its grip when spring comes again."

I see the young woman in the Widow then, and the love that makes her long to keep her son. I feel her anguish, for that is how my father must feel every day.

The ribbons hang in front of me, their colors blurring into a dangling gray. I cannot decide, but the pedlar chooses yellow for me, and he will not take the coin I offer him.

The buds swell in the orchard. In the lane, daffodils splash their yellow against the muddy grass. Lambs bleat on the hills. I count the celandines, the primroses, the crocuses, the church days: Shrove Tuesday, Ash Wednesday, Christ crucified, Christ alive again, Christ risen to Heaven.

Hester packs a marriage chest for me. While I have

thought of nothing but Tom, she has provided everything I might miss in my land – and things I can take back to my people. I weep at her kindness, for she has chosen well for me: scissors, thimbles, pins, needles, cotton thread, buttons. And clothes as if for a new bride – embroidered nightshifts, gloves, ruffs, cloth to make dresses and all the shoes I have already worn. They must have cost her dear, not only in money, but in tears. And enough ribbons to last the rest of my life.

And household things: cups, spoons, a kettle, plates and knives, which I'll share with Tom.

The sails of the *Lion* show on the horizon just after the sun has set. Now we have two days to wait, the worst two days of my life. Hester cannot be consoled. Neither can the Widow. I have little to say to Master White.

I do not see Tom until we are waiting by the small boat, where Master Henry and Francis embrace us both with sudden warmth.

And so we set sail to my land – to Virginia.

A roll of drums, a cannon boom. Mist hides the church tower. I cannot look back any longer. As I fix my eyes on the *Lion,* I hear my father's warning in the wind:

Keep away from them, Nadie. They want to take our women to breathe life back into themselves. They are bloodless. Their hair hangs from their faces. They foul the water that we drink. What creature would do that?

Can I take Tom to him?

And next to me, Tom is covering his ears to drown out the sound of his mother's cries. The sun comes out, but it does not reach the fear that each of us has buried deep inside.

A World Away

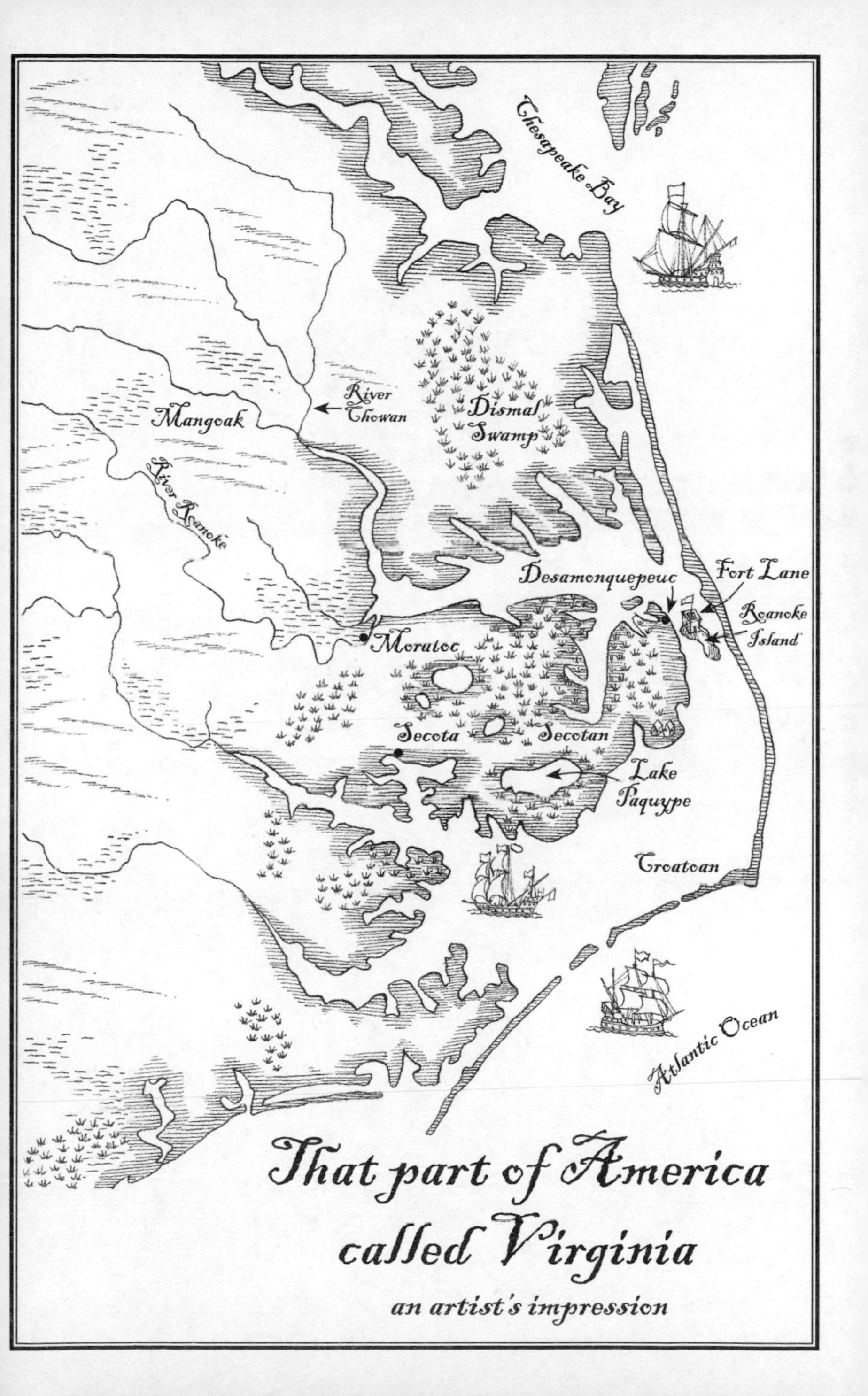
Chesapeake Bay
River Chowan
Mangoak
Dismal Swamp
River Roanoke
Desamonquepeuc
Fort Lane
Roanoke Island
Moratoc
Secota
Secotan
Lake Paquype
Croatoan
Atlantic Ocean
That part of America called Virginia
an artist's impression

Roanoke Island, The Americas, 1587

Tom

What have I done?

Roanoke Island rises in the twilight. Thin clouds dampen our faces with drizzle. Birds fly low over the creeks, fearing a storm as lightning forks the gloom.

The horror of the voyage has hardly left me. We sailed from Plymouth on the seventh day of May and first sighted the Virginian coast on the sixteenth of July. The wind still shrieks in my ears, the sea still swells and sickens me.

I reach for Nadie's hand, but she hardly notices. Her eyes are looking beyond the island toward the mainland. There, a river glints under the rising moon. Toward the horizon, where the river dims, lies nothing but darkening forest, and, here and there, the glow of a small fire from hidden villages.

We've already cheered as we reached the outer islands, and prayed as we navigated the dangerous sand shoals with their churning channels that brought us closer to Roanoke. Now we gulp down our celebration ration of ale.

"I reckon we're the only ones who'll be any use," I say. My words slur. "We'll be the ones working our fingers to the bone. Where's Master White been all this time, then? He's been dining on fine silver with the gentlemen who've paid to come with him."

"Aye, he'll be standing on that shore soon, unrolling his piece of parchment..." Will clears his throat. "I do declare...I do declare on this twenty-third day of July in the year of our Lord 1587, I, John White do set foot in the New World as Governor of the City of Raleigh, in the state of Virginia. I promise to serve Her Most

Gracious Majesty, Queen Elizabeth the First, Defender of the Faith..."

"Don't mock him, husband," Mary says. "He wants this colony to survive. Why else would he have brought his own daughter? She's almost six months with child. That's a brave thing to do."

"Mary had a bad time birthing Joshua," Will says. "I worry what'll happen if she has another child. I've heard your women give birth with little fuss, Nadie."

She doesn't hear him. "You can see Desamonquepeuc from here, where Wingina lived...and the River Roanoke. We call it the Long Man because its head is in the mountains and its feet in the great salt water. Secota, my village, lies on a wide creek, where the sun sets, but it is too far away to see."

I want her to stop talking, to stop saying the names of her land – names that end with the click of her tongue, that have none of the softness of Devon. They frighten me.

When we kneel on deck for evening prayer and thank God for our safe delivery, I pray only for myself and Nadie, not for the City of Raleigh.

Am I no better than Raleigh? A dreamer, who can't

cope with the real world? A dreamer who's allowed my head to be filled with promises?

I long for morning light to lift the shadows. Then I remember.

Tomorrow, my real journey begins.

Impatience grips me. I want to set foot on my land again, and I would have already swum to shore if it had not been for Tom, although he is so lost in his own world that he does not see how restless I am.

I lean over the edge of the *Lion.* Where are my people? Why do they not come to greet us?

A canoe is outlined against the sky, making for the creek. I call out my greeting, but there is no reply.

When I kneel with them, my prayer is to the gods,

thanking them for bringing me home, for bringing me Tom.

I have already forgotten the sea storms and salted beef, and the islands of the Caribbean, where the world was new to both of us, where my eyes feasted on leaping fish and lush green, and people as dark-skinned as I am. Yes, all forgotten in the magic of homecoming.

Poor Tom! He is trembling like a newborn. I remember that day on the Plymouth waterside, kicking and biting, and I hold his hand. Then I think: He *chose* to come.

Tomorrow, I touch my land again.

Tom

Daylight welcomes us with drifting clouds in a blue sky. Roanoke's bathed in sunshine, its trees inviting us into their shade.

None of us has slept well. Voices shouted all through the night, those of Master White and our navigator, Fernandez. We prepare to land on Roanoke Island to fetch the soldiers from Fort Lane, and to find fresh food and water. Nadie and I are in the first boat to leave – forty of us, keen to feel land under our feet.

By noon, we're all crammed onto a narrow stretch of sand – over a hundred of us – swaying to an invisible ship, craning our necks for sight of the fort and the soldiers left behind last year.

But Master White's brooding with anger.

I have touched my land.

I kick off my shoes and peel off my stockings, tie up the hem of my dress. I would put on my deerskin skirt if I did not dislike the pale men's eyes on my breasts.

Lifting my arms to the sun, I whisper to the spirits in the rocks and rivers, in the trees and reeds, ask them to forgive me for leaving them, and I hear their sighs in the wind as they welcome me home.

There are fleeting shadows among the trees, the

shadows of my people who dare not show themselves. Fear has come to my land, as surely as blight to the corn, the fear that new terror could strike at any time, and that is the worst fear of all.

Master White's voice hardly cuts through my thoughts, but, when I turn around, the colonists are gazing across the water at the *Lion*. They are fearful, too. They want to go back.

And I did not know how much I wanted to come home. Master White was right.

Tom

Master White's voice rages above the roar of the waves. "We shall not sail on to Chesapeake Bay. The City of Raleigh will grow on these shores." He picks up a stone and hurls it into the water. "Fernandez is the very devil! He has refused to take us north. He wants us settled now, so that he can return to England before the autumn storms. That is mutiny, in my eyes. But I have no choice...he..."

"But how can we stay here?" Mistress Payne

interrupts, "after what happened last year? You killed their chief, have you forgotten?" She turns to us, her eyes alight with brief madness. "We're doomed. We're *all* doomed!"

"Be silent, Mistress," Master White snaps. "I do not allow such thoughts in my colony. Now, let us make for Fort Lane before nightfall. *Concordia parva crescunt.*"

"Speak plain English, man!" a voice calls. I turn around. It's Jack, the tin miner from Cornwall. He glowers.

"Small things increase," Master White answers. He glares at Jack. "Strength in unity, boy."

Nadie's eyes are bright with happiness when I tell her, for she'll be closer to her people. I felt such love for her when she stepped ashore that my heart's still bursting. I'll take my strength from her, make her proud of me.

She wanted to come home, but she would have stayed in Plymouth for me.

Fort Lane stands on the north of Roanoke Island. It was built two years ago, when Master White first came to Virginia, and named for the captain – Captain Lane

– who came with him. We follow the shore at first, hauling the heavy carts like horses. Then we tramp through stinking swamps, where mosquitoes swarm like black clouds, where clams crackle under our feet. I shiver, although the sun beats down. Nobody admits it, but the thought lies over us like a rain cloud: we'll be pleased to see the fifteen soldiers, to see the metal of their muskets. We're settlers, not soldiers. We sing sea songs, whistle, bang sticks to warn them, but also to make us feel braver.

Nadie walks ahead. Then she signs us to stop. Master White makes his musket ready and runs forward, telling me to follow with Will and his son-in-law, Ananias Dare. A skeleton lies in the sand, its empty eye sockets looking at the sky, its face in that eternal grimace that fleshless faces have. Wisps of blond hair blow across its bony temples. Rotting arrows poke from its ribs, and other arrows lie beside it.

He must have been killed by one of Nadie's people, and if his fellow soldiers have left him unburied, it means that...

My thoughts sicken me, and I fight to keep control.

We found a dead sheep once, Francis and I, in a field beyond Plymouth wall. He poked it with a stick and flies flew into his face and the more he screamed, the more they buzzed into his mouth, until he was sick and they left him to feast on that. It was the first time I'd ever seen him lose control, and it frightened me.

We scoop in the sandy dust, as Nadie cradles the bones. Then we place them in the shallow hollow. Nobody mentions the arrowheads that still lie in the sand. We bury those, too.

When Master White's said the Lord's Prayer, we all walk on, sick at heart and silent. I lift little Joshua, Mary's son, onto my shoulders, calling out the sights to him; but in truth, I'm now frightened of every shadow and leaf, wincing at the wind, expecting it to be a swish of arrows.

We all fear what we'll find at Fort Lane. As we glimpse a roof through the trees, we hear the pattering of feet and the rustling of leaves. We walk the last steps in silence. The buildings no longer look like English houses. Their roofs and upper floors need repair. Vines, heavy with melons and early grapes, twist through the lower windows. Bright blue flowers blink at us. Deer have trampled the rotting palisade and graze, or reach for the fruit.

They scatter at our approach.

We pull away the undergrowth, snap and chop branches growing through the roofs, nervous as we search for more bodies. But there's nobody there, although armor and firearms still lie in rotting chests inside the houses. Master White makes the sign of the cross. "Lord have mercy on them!"

Three thousand miles for what? To find our countrymen fled or worse? One dead, and fourteen *where*?

The need for food and fresh water distracts us, but, with nightfall, the fear comes again. I can feel it in everybody around me. I felt it when my father died: heart hammering, hands sweating, bowels loosening. We glance toward the outer islands, and take strength from the *Lion* lying at anchor.

Master White speaks at length before our evening prayers. "Christ came into Jerusalem on a donkey. We have come to the New World on a ship, not to convert, but to make a new life for ourselves. We may go hungry. We may have to fashion food from five loaves and two small fishes."

"There's more than two fishes in these waters," Will calls out and we laugh.

"The people came to welcome *Him* with palm leaves," Master White continues. "There is no such welcome for us. We must be patient. Remember the last time we came. We burned and killed. We must pray for forgiveness." He glances at Nadie. "We shall move to the mainland before the winter storms, but before that, we must make our peace with the people who live there. I shall be sending messages to the people of Secota and Desamonquepeuc, asking their forgiveness for the death of their chief Wingina, begging them to start afresh in new friendship. Meanwhile, go nowhere alone. We want peace, but we must know that we can overpower the people here at anytime, whenever we wish. Shoot to instill fear if you must, but do not use your weapons to kill."

Nadie frowns. "My people can fire an arrow quicker than you can load your musket. But they do not fight unless it is to defend themselves." Her voice is sharp with anger. "They are in the fields now, cutting corn. We know how to feed ourselves." She sighs. "I want to see my people, speak to them, even if you do not. There is a village close by, where our great chief Wingina used to live before you came. But they are afraid to show themselves because of you."

We look away from her, ashamed, and in the silence, Joyce Payne raises her voice in a hymn.

It shows on their faces in the morning sun – relief at having survived the night. Do they think my people are all murdering savages?

There are twelve Assistants in our colony, each responsible for the care and good behavior of about twenty people. Like the twelve disciples, Mary says. They strut, displaying their coats of arms, muskets swinging from their shoulders. They are young and old, and they can all read and write; but they have their own pecking order. The older men are fair in their dealings with us. The younger ones, who are less experienced, try to exert their authority through strictness. Some of them are gentlemen, who have paid dearly to come here in the hope of finding gold, pearls and copper. They are the ones who grumble at the lack of soft beds and good food and waste their days in idleness.

Our Assistant is called Master Cooper, and he has traveled alone. He is red-haired and red-skinned and always squinting in the sun, although his wide-brimmed hat shades his face. His voice is as thin as the wind in the reeds. I want to breathe life into him with the bellows. He scribbles constantly on his scraps of parchment. Why does he have to write down all that he sees?

Since we found the skeleton, the colonists do not trust me. In Plymouth, Abigail and Tom's mother cursed me, it is true, but most people only came to gawp because they knew no better. Most of my unhappiness came from my grief. Can they not imagine what it is like for me, knowing my father is only a few days' walk away?

But now the stakes are higher. I think these people hold me responsible for whether they survive or not, and this is too big a burden for me to bear. I have had so many these last moons.

Dread fills me, dampening the love that burns between me and Tom. And so I draw into myself, apart from them, and when I go into the forest to be alone, they do not like it. They think I am going to give my people an account of their numbers and weapons.

Although the sky is clear, it seems full of clouds casting their shadow over me, and, when they are too dark, I find Joshua. He is truly happy, dangling his legs over the muddy inlets, scraps of salted beef at the end of a rope to catch crabs. He knows that if he throws the small ones back, he will have a better catch in the future.

My people do not often show their grief in tears. My shoulders shake as I weep, dry-eyed, and, seeing no tears, Joshua thinks that I am laughing and leaves his fishing line to show me his cartwheels. I watch his feet, golden against the sun, and beg the gods to show me a happy path.

Dear Mary sees my unhappiness and asks me to show her how to plait mats for the floors and windows and the fishing weirs, how to recognize fruits and vegetables and fish. She makes the houses bright with scented honeysuckles and cozy with her marriage linen. My fingers are raw from weaving the reeds. I do not like doing this again. I have grown used to soft hands.

How difficult it is to wait.

A musket shot calls us to prayers at dusk, for this is a godly colony, where the open air is our church. But I fear that the shots will terrify my people, or be used against them if they happen to run from the trees.

Master White soothes me. "We shall not soak this soil with their blood. We shall work for what we need here, not steal from your people with threats of shot and sword."

"Have you sent your men to my people?"

"Yes, Nadie. They will ask your chiefs to come within the week to talk of peace."

But I want to go to Secota now.

Tom

Lighting the forge fire on the shore has calmed me. It took two of us to lift the anvil from the cart.

"A smith should shift his own anvil!" Ananias Dare shouts. I hate him for it, but it's true. My body's weak after the voyage. The sea took all the strength from me.

The fire must be fed, but fetching the wood terrifies me. Instead of choosing old trees, I chop saplings because it's quicker. I'm used to city walls and gates and a safe harbor.

I learned on the *Lion* that there was no master blacksmith in the colony to supervise me. I was angry then, because Master White lied to me. But now that I'm here, it bothers me little, for I'm used to working alone. My apprenticeship seems as out of reach as Plymouth itself. And what *is* there to make, except door hinges and bolts and hooks, and repair the pots and pans?

There aren't many rules on Roanoke: a head count at dusk, to find firewood, food and fish in fives. One rule carries the punishment of death: no stealing of food rations. We don't understand at first. We've oysters as big as apples, more lobsters and fish than we can eat, more fruit than we can pick: strawberries, cranberries, huckleberries and prickly pears.

And one unspoken rule: we are each responsible for the food we find here, and if we don't find it, we won't eat anything but rations.

I don't like our Assistant. I'm not used to such men, men who don't soil their hands. He uses words I don't always understand. He works with his head. I work with my hands.

But we all work together to repair the fort. We use tree trunks for the walls, lugging them back to the fort by hand, missing the horses to pull our carts. We intertwine them with branches, and weave reeds for the roof. Master Dare works fast, for he's a master tiler and sure of his footing. The floors are brushed and flattened earth, sprinkled with small orange flowers that grow everywhere.

Everybody works, except Agnes. Although she sits in the shade, she still protects her skin with her shawl, wiping her face, whimpering every time a bird squawks or an animal scuttles across her feet.

"Get up, Aggie!" Mary scolds her sister, as she would Joshua. "Do *something*. There's the fire to watch. There's the pot to stir."

If Agnes moves, it's to circle me like they say the moon circles the earth, as if I can give her strength. She becomes my shadow. And if my voice is too sharp, her eyes brim and her lower lip slackens like a child's. Then Nadie tosses her hair and sighs.

Those first days are like a summer feast. More fish than we can eat roasted over the fire on sticks with onions and Devon apples from the barrel. Turtles and tortoises give us their eggs. Lobsters and oysters. Berries for the picking. And I wake up every morning knowing that I'll see Nadie all day. I watch her – skirts pulled up, searching for lobster with Joshua, slicing off the tail spike they'll use later as a fishing spear.

But there are no secret meetings, no stolen kisses through the steam of the forge. We're never alone as we were in Back Lane. I want her more than ever, and I've come all this way for her; but she's slipping away from me. I ask Master White if I can take her to Secota. He shakes his head, insisting that we wait for her people to come here to talk of peace.

"Nadie will protect me, sir."

"You cannot be sure of that, Tom." He casts his eyes over Fort Lane, its new roofs rising against the trees.

"So Nadie's our hostage," I say.

"I would not use that word." Master White straightens himself and the musket on his shoulder rattles. "And who are you to question me in this way when I gave you a chance?" He must have seen the anguish in my eyes, for he says, "If you want my advice, secure Nadie now. She can be baptized when my grandchild is born. Then you can wed afterward. Do you think she is ready to give up her gods?"

I shake my head.

"But she will expect you to forget our God. Take care, Tom. If you marry according to her custom, you will be living in sin. You will be outcasts in the colony."

"I may not think about God very much, sir, but I'm mindful of the law. I've grown up with boys who were born out of wedlock, and it makes them wild. I wouldn't want that for my child."

He seems distracted. "The Indian is like a fox in the wood. We need them to trade with if we are to survive the winter."

"But they don't need us," I reply.

I seek out Nadie on the shore, telling her what Master White's said. "Where are my people, who should come to talk of peace?" she cries. Then her face hardens. "But why should they come just because *your* people have commanded it?"

I take her hand, and we follow bird tracks to the sand, and shells creak under our feet. Birds preen and snooze at the water's edge, becoming a silver shower when flight reveals their white markings. Rivulets of water run between my toes, chilling me. And, sometimes, the sun comes out and chases away the shadows from her face.

In six days, the time it took God to create the world, we created the City of Raleigh. But we don't rest on the seventh day. One of the Assistants, George Howe, is missing at evening prayer.

We search the houses and the outlying grass; but he's not there. We search the shore. We walk to the north. Then we search the swampy creeks two miles to the south. We take off our shoes and wade into the reeds. And that's where we find him, lying in the bulrushes, bare-headed and bare-chested, beaten so badly that we hardly know him. Sixteen arrows have pierced his skin.

"Now we are paying for Wingina's death," Master White says.

Fear fills every bird cry, every animal shriek. Before, we kept close to Nadie. She was our lucky charm, the one who would keep us safe, the bridge between our world and hers. Some shun her openly now. I watched Eleanor yesterday. She should know better. Nadie came back with a lobster for her, but Eleanor refused to take it. I was ashamed for Master White, that his own daughter should be so hostile to her.

At first, we all looked better on Roanoke. Faces brown, clothes loosened, relaxed after the confinement of the voyage out. But now I see a faint hollowing of the cheeks, a watchful look in the eyes, a tension shown by a twitching cheek or mouth. I've seen it in horses all my life, when they first come to be shod. Nervous in new places, they prick up their ears at the slightest sound.

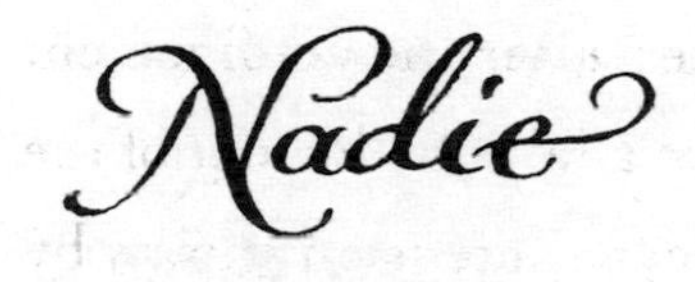

My dreams are bright with flames, waking me before dawn. In the gathering light, thick smoke rises over Desamonquepeuc. The boat is missing from the waterside. Master White and twenty others are not at morning prayers.

I cannot stay still, checking the fishing weirs, making candles – anything to keep me calm. The sun climbs. My heart tightens.

The boat returns from the mainland around noon,

low in the water, laden with corn, squash and tobacco leaves. I smile. They have been to trade for food. Then I see that Master Dare's shirtsleeves are smeared with blood.

My heart thuds.

They come ashore in silence, eyes not meeting ours as we gather around them.

"How many did you kill, sir?" I ask.

"We could wait no longer," Master White says. "Our deadline for peace talks has passed. We cannot tolerate the death of George Howe. We went to find those who killed him. We took them by surprise, at dawn when they were sitting around the fire. There will be no more trouble."

"How many did you kill?"

"Only one. The others ran into the reeds."

"You've given them what they feared most," Mary cries. "A bullet! How can we live in peace after this?"

"Hold your tongue, Mistress Lucas."

Pain shoots through my heart. I pick up the knife that lies next to the fire. Agnes shouts, "Savage!" The men on the roof stop their work, slide down to the ground, holding up saws and hammers. I throw off my cap, take the hair that falls across my face and cut it so that it settles just above my eyes. My voice rages. "This is how the women of my land wear their hair. If you come here, you must see us as we really are!" I walk closer to Master White. "Do you see me *now*? Open your hearts to us, or you will not survive. Open your minds, or you will live in ignorance. You have betrayed me, Master White. You put right the wrong your people did to me, but now you have done an even greater wrong. *Why?*"

"Calm yourself, Nadie." Master White tries to touch my arm, but he flinches at the glint of my knife. "I gave your people seven days to bring me their answer."

"Who are *you* to tell *us* what to do?" I stamp the ground. "I pray for the mighty Thunderbird to carry you away for what you have done. Take care, Master White, they send lightning bolts if you break a promise. And there are creatures under the sea as dangerous as those that live on the land, and if they come out to fight the Thunderbirds, there will be raging storms and floods and..."

They all back away, fearful, their faces hostile. Master Dare levels his musket.

"Savage!" Agnes shouts again. She has run to the safety of Will and Mary.

"It is your people who are savages," I say. Only the fire lies between us. In that moment, I face them alone. "Shoot *me*. But your bullet will not strike me in the back. Look into my eyes as you send it."

As the flames spark, Tom pushes Master Dare aside and comes through the smoke to take my hand. Eleanor comes to Master White's side, her feet unsteady under her swollen belly. Her mouth twists with dislike as she looks at Tom through the thinning smoke. "My father has treated you like his own son," she says. "Did he not tell you about his firstborn who died...*his* Thomas?"

Tom only stares at her father. "I'll take Nadie home," he says.

"NO." Master White raises his musket, too. "You are forgetting yourself, Master Martyn. I am the Governor of the City of Raleigh. You are subject to the law of Her Majesty, Queen Elizabeth the First. If you desert, you will be shot."

“I can wait, Tom.” I stare at Master White, until he shifts, uneasy. “It is something I learned to do in your land, sir.”

The tension dissolves. Master White nods and puts away his musket. Master Dare does the same and, suddenly, all is bustle again. Agnes and Mary bring more water for the pot. The men return to their hammering on the roof. Master White goes to the boat to divide the spoils.

It is never talked of again. But some of the women nod as I pass and ask my advice. And I thank my mother for moulding me into a strong pot which refuses to break.

Tom

I can't forgive Master White for what he's done to Nadie's people. And I'm left to mutter my dark thoughts.

Eleanor's daughter is born, lifting our spirits. For a few days, all is well again. The sun blazes, the baby thrives, we catch as much fish as we need and pick oysters and walnuts as big as eggs. The birds and crickets sing. And for a time, we forget that the *Lion* is preparing to return to Plymouth. Why did Fernandez refuse to sail on, then lie at anchor for so long?

Aye, this is still paradise – except that Eleanor won't let Nadie hold her baby. I can hardly bear the loving looks that pass between Eleanor and her husband. I beg Nadie again to be baptized with their baby, who'll be named Virginia, and marry me afterward – but her eyes fill with anger.

"Why should I trust your God, who allows my people to be murdered again and again?" she asks. "Now you must trust me and wait until I have taken you to my father."

I've no answer.

The summer cools early. The change is subtle as the greens fade. Master White watches, hand shading his eyes, like an artist standing back from his canvas, like a man who wants to paint the green back.

Gossip spreads like the plague. The supply ships from England will search for us at Chesapeake Bay. *Ergo...* somebody must go back to England on the *Lion* and tell Raleigh that we're at Roanoke, for nobody trusts Fernandez now. The Assistants vote that Master White must take responsibility as the Governor of the City of Raleigh. *Ergo,* he must sail, although he doesn't want to.

He strides up and down the shore, looking out to the *Lion.* But I've no pity for him. Sometimes, Eleanor leads him back to the shade and places Virginia in his arms.

Then the wind shifts. It blows raw from the north-east, whipping the water high, howling as it gains strength. The water froths at our feet. The *Lion* moves out to sea and waits at anchor. When sunlight touches the sand again, Fernandez sends a stark message: he will sail on the next tide.

"So your curse is upon us!" Eleanor says to Nadie. "My father should have sent you to Secota as soon as we landed." She starts to cry. "Now he won't see baby Virginia's first smile. He might never see her again."

Master White's more concerned for his paints than his people. He buries them with his armor inside the fort. Those who can write send short notes, which the Assistants read before they're sealed, for we must say nothing against this paradise, if Raleigh's to supply Virginia. I'm relieved that Nadie must write my letter for me, for my nervousness now that the ship's leaving would surely show in the trembling of my hand.

We gather around the boat, buffeted by the wind.

Master White shouts above its shrieking. "Our rations are running low, and even if I return immediately with supplies, you cannot survive the winter. You must move to the mainland before the winter storms and trade with the villages. Do not let these people think you are desperate or you will give everything, but receive little in return. Scatter to survive, for no village can feed all of you. There is good land north by the River Chowon, where Master Lane went. There are friendly people on Croatoan Island. But remember that wherever you go, you are still my colony. Master Cooper, you will take Nadie to her people, with as many others as wish to go with you. But come back to Roanoke for the supply ship in the spring. I shall see you all next year, God willing. And, until then, I leave you safe in His hands."

He kisses his daughter and baby Virginia – and he would have kissed Nadie if she hadn't backed away. As he climbs into the boat, I grip her hand to stop me going after him.

We came here full of hope, barely two months ago. Now our colony must survive alone.

I hold my breath until the *Lion* is a glinting speck. Agnes throws herself onto the sand, skirts flying over her head, and tears at her hair. But Will shrugs as Mary runs to her sister.

These people are in a dream all day. Like shipwrecked souls, they look in horror at the space where their ship was anchored. They blink hard, sigh and carry on. I soften toward them. They have had the courage to give up what they know to settle in a new land. They do not beg to go back, even if they could, for they have paid dearly to come here. Now that Tom has come all this way for me, I must protect him as he protected me in Plymouth.

The sun is losing its fiery red under pale mists. The children play closer to their mothers as the sea lashes, not lulls. The danger will not come from my people.

"Tom, the song of the cricket is changing," I tell him. "We must move before the cold moons."

Tom

A harvest moon without a harvest, rising soon after sunset, then full and low in the sky. Our moment of truth. The moon is full but we are not.

The wind from the sea freshens each day, the moon now lies slender on its back as if resting after the toil of harvest and the cold sharpens into night frost before we know it. The blue sky's deceived us. But as a reward, it gives us a leaf color we've never seen before under the cloudy English sky. The colors are startling: oak leaves the color of copper, hickory leaves golden brown, the maples scarlet and yellow.

But the sea's lashing at our door.

Most of those who boarded the *Lion* in Plymouth – who knew Nadie there – decide to come with us to Secota. Will, Mary and Joshua. Agnes. Rose and Henry Chapman. Jack and Edward. Joyce and John Payne, a goldsmith and his brother and family, a clerk from Tiverton. Nineteen of us, for Master Cooper will lead us.

We bury some of our boxes inside the fort, along with Master White's. I'm not ashamed to admit it. I kiss the anvil before I bury it, let its metal cool my cheeks for a moment before I drop it into the hole. Joshua cries to leave his friends, and Eleanor and Agnes embrace each other long after we've said goodbye. Part of me is glad to be leaving the others. I don't like the way they've treated Nadie. She's glad, too. I see her shoulders relax, her face lose its wary look. But part of me knows this is the most difficult thing I've ever done. It was easy to love her in Plymouth. It's easy to love her in her land amongst my own people.

Now I've got to face her people.

I tighten the rope on the handcart. Across the narrow water lies the wilderness. I must prove myself in Nadie's land. I can't call it Virginia anymore.

We wave as the small boat returns to Roanoke Island. Then we turn our backs to the water.

Only then do I realize that I have never walked the path to my village. Why should I? I have been to Roanoke only in my father's canoe. At the place where the River Roanoke flows into the salt water, we turn toward the sunset.

But how can I walk in the place where the blood of Wingina was spilled without my tears spilling, too?

We skirt around Desamonquepeuc for I cannot be sure of what my people might do. My heart fills with anger for the pale people who follow me, and they know it. When we have left the village behind, Master Cooper halts us.

"Listen. Our people brought death to Nadie's chief. Could we forgive an assassin of our most Gracious Majesty, the Queen Elizabeth, as Nadie has forgiven us? Let us kneel and pray for forgiveness and that God may relieve Nadie's despair."

This act of kindness dissolves the knot of misery inside me. I do not try to hide my tears this time. I weep for a long time, and they let me.

And my heart is lighter.

Then we set off again, tramping through shallow water, dense with oak trees, willows, maples.

"Will there be people like you?" Joshua asks.

"I hope so," I say.

They walk with care, like hunted prey. They are as nervous as the deer on Roanoke. They are so *slow*!

Soon, I am ahead. I am used to walking fast. It is something my people do well because they have no carts or horses. We hold ourselves straight and step out, almost on tiptoe, unlike the pale people who are uncertain and heavy-footed. But they run to catch up with me, for I am their lucky charm again.

Impatience fills me. These people, who have just shown me such kindness, irritate me like midges on my skin. They are slowing me down with their cart, their grumbling and their groaning – and their fear, which presses on them so hard they can hardly walk. Without them, I could run all the way.

Agnes is always startled, for she fears lions and tigers. There are no tigers in my land, and lions only live in the far-off mountains, but I do not tell her that. The others do, but she wants to hear it from my lips, I know.

Let her be afraid.

Then I remember that first time in St. Andrew's church, when I screamed to the rafters at the sight of the eagle, and I feel shame. I go back to Agnes and tell her there are no such creatures, and she murmurs her thanks.

Doubt walks with me all the way. How will these pale people persuade my people to part with their food for the cold moons? By offering another cooking pot?

Some of the Secotan men want muskets, for there are other tribes beyond the River Roanoke who desire our land. What better way to fight them?

My thoughts exhaust me as much as the journey exhausts those with me, and I am glad that Master Cooper calls a halt when darkness falls. We all sink gratefully into sleep, leaving Will and Tom to watch the fire. When the darkness is deep, it vibrates with howling. Poor Agnes! I did not warn her about the wolves.

It is three days since we left Roanoke and I am weary of them all, even Tom. Like stones, they hang around my neck, pulling me toward dark thoughts.

Will my father see beyond what happened last year and let me marry Tom? Will he accept that I shall have to leave my people again to live in the colony, for this is the promise Tom made to Master White? With such thoughts, my courage almost deserts me.

Water gleams through the trees. This is the great water without salt – Paquype – where I came for my vision quest. A thousand hoofs thunder in my head, my heartbeat quickens, and I know that I am meant to be with Tom. Why else would the horse have taken me to his forge?

The water is full of fish and fowl. The pink of herons' legs flashes against the dusk, and geese, our guests for the cold moons, cackle on the shore.

Tomorrow, we shall come to Secota. "Prepare your feast, Father," I whisper. "I am coming home."

I know my people are watching us from the trees. I call out to them, telling them to send word to my father: that Nadie – *onida,* the lost one – has come back.

Tom

Nadie's as changeable as the autumn winds that whip us as we walk, sometimes salty from the sea, sometimes scented from the forest.

We depend on her, and she knows it. I want to shout at her to slow down, but I don't, for the cart's heavy to pull. Agnes rests on it, and Joshua lies against her, wrapped in my blanket, flushed with fever.

Sighted from Roanoke Island, this land seemed untouched, a true wilderness, but now I know it isn't true. To my surprise, there are stretches of land that've been cleared by fire, and they look like English fields after the corn stubble's been burned.

I fear Nadie's father more than I fear this land. She's warned me: wait for her father to speak; don't offer him gifts; don't contradict him; greet him in his tongue. And let her do the talking. I've no choice in that, for I've learned only a few words of her tongue.

The lake lifts our spirits. It's beautiful. The sun's already dipping as we light the fire. Hares and squirrels dart among the trees and, for a moment, I think I'm back in Devon. Golden maple leaves shimmer with spiders' webs in the firelight.

"There's gold where there's spiders' webs," Edward says.

Jack scoffs. "Then why ain't there any gold in England?" he says. "It's teeming with spiders."

"We do not want gold," Master Cooper protests. "It brings grief to all men. In the land to the south, in Florida, the Spanish stole so much of it that two of the natives poured liquid gold down the throats of the Spanish thieves. There is a painting in—"

Mary frowns. "That's enough, Master Cooper," she says.

"Soon you will see my people and know that you have nothing to fear," Nadie says. She smiles at me for the first time since we left Roanoke. I like the new happiness on her face. It gives me hope, too. But the enormity of what I'm doing makes my heart somersault. What will her father want from me?

He will not know until he has seen you with his own eyes, Nadie said.

My mind runs on. Shall I have to fight with a Secotan man who loves Nadie as much as I do? Shall I have to face a trial by fire as I walk over hot coals? Shall I have to shoot an arrow through an apple thrown into the air?

No. Such things only happen in the stories Francis used to read to me. And I must leave them where they belong – in my childhood.

Secota is beyond the next creek.

My pace quickens. I run past the inlet where I used to swim with my father, past the hollow oaks where I collected wild honey. I glimpse the fields of tobacco. Then, closer, fields of sunflowers, swaying over me, their petals still perfect, their brown eyes glistening with ripe seeds. I link my arms around the tallest and pull its face toward mine and kiss it. Tom catches up with me and laughs. Birds, pecking their crusty seeds, startle into flight as I shake one of the heads, catch the seeds and cram them into my mouth.

Yes, my people are among the trees – I can smell them.

I need not hurry. I have waited fifteen moons to come home.

Tom

Our mouths hang open. Nadie's people surround us, about twenty of them.

The Secotan men are tall and straight. Their backs aren't bent from hunching over the anvil. They carry bows as tall as themselves, and arrows almost as long, some tipped with stone, some with birds' claws. Bones and animal teeth dangle from their ears and around their necks. The women are dressed like Nadie when she came to Plymouth. They rush forward, calling out her name. Nadie runs to meet them and the women embrace her and stroke her face, weeping.

The men swarm around us, buzzing like flies, touching the cart, running their hands around the rims of its wheels. Naked children chase Joshua, who is suddenly shy and clings to his mother, but they come to touch him anyway.

Nadie walks with her people, passing the ripe corn, where a boy perches on a platform to scare away birds and deer.

I let her go ahead. I must be patient, for she's suffered so much. We lift the handles of the cart and follow, the dogs snapping around our aching legs. I wipe my face and teeth, smooth down my hair, glad that my skin's dark, wish that my eyes were brown, wish that I was wearing my blacksmith's apron.

And we're there.

The village perches on the edge of the creek, surrounded by fields bursting with corn, beans twining around their stalks. It's bigger than I expected. About ten houses are scattered around a street swept smooth, their roofs layered with bark and leaves. A fire, built high, supports an earthenware pot. Three women squat around it, and, as they stir the contents with a stick, the smell of fish and vegetables reaches us. That is the only smell, unlike the stench of Fort Lane, where we feared to go into the forest to relieve ourselves.

Nadie isn't crying when I catch up with her, although her eyes are shining. Her breath comes quickly with little gasps of pleasure.

"*Onida* no more," she says.

The Assistant suddenly strides past me. He tries to shake me off as I pull him back, but I hold onto him, forcing him to let Nadie lead us to her people.

I walk past the place where my mother fell, my shoes crunching on the brittle bark. There is silence, except for the dogs barking and the swish of leaves overhead. In Plymouth, people called out to me and tried to touch me. Those who embraced me by the sunflowers now keep their distance. I call out my greeting.

Perhaps they think *I* have come back from the dead.

I have never seen them so still. Where is my friend, Amitola? I have ribbons for her in my box, but I dare not take them out. Where is my cousin, Seekanauk? Did he survive in the river that day?

Where is my *father*?

No drum beating. No clapping. No singing.

No harvest celebration, although the baskets are heaped high with corn.

Nothing.

Our village chief, Manchese, is squatting by the fire, in conversation with the elders, all staring into the flames. Only our wise man, who whispers with them, watches me, his eyes half hidden by the dead black bird that perches across his right ear. Husks of corn scatter the ground. Clay plates are piled to one side. I smooth my ragged dress, tug at my fringe. And all the time, I search their solemn faces. Then I see Seekanauk, squatting on the steps of his house, but he looks away from me.

At last, my father shows himself. He is walking toward me, his finger pointing as if he wants to poke out my eyes. I run, arms outstretched, but I stop as he holds up his hand. His eyes are full of anger. The setting sun deepens the folds of his face. We stare at each other in the evening shadows, like animals poised to attack. How I have longed for this moment! He looks me up and down, disgust distorting his mouth. He touches my dress, but he does not touch me. I try to embrace him, but he pushes me away.

This cannot be happening.

His eyes narrow. "You have brought shame on your family, daughter. You have struck terror into us because you only think of yourself. We heard of your pale people walking through the forest. We heard that you were coming back. Yes, you have betrayed us, bringing them *here*."

My smile fades. Suddenly, I am looking at him across a gulf, greater than the great salt water that I crossed.

"Have you no pity for me?" I cry. The words of my tongue seem strange at first. Then they tumble out, more precious now than before. "Snatched from all I knew and taken across the great salt water? I did not *ask* to go! Do you not wonder what *my* life has been like since then?"

Chief Manchese comes to join my father. The red circles painted on his arms and chest remind me of the bloodstains on Master Dare's shirtsleeves. I kneel. Master Cooper has come to stand behind me, and I am pleased that he is there. The evening breeze gathers strength, whistling through the trees. Master Cooper puts down his musket, takes off his cap, and bows, asking me to tell my chief that they have brought me back as soon as they could, that the pale men are sorry for taking me.

Manchese thanks him. Then he looks to the others huddled under the trees. "Daughter of Secota, how can we ever forget the first coming of the pale men, for the day turned to night and the wind howled? The curse of that dark day has never left us. Why have you brought the people who murdered Wingina, and who still murder?"

"It is not their fault. These are good people, who want to live here in peace. *They* also know what it is like to live in fear. Their enemies are building ships to come and take their land. It was their chief, Master White... the man who came to make paintings of Secota...who decided to go to Desamonquepeuc. We did not know what he was going to do."

"But what are they doing *here*?"

"They arrived in our land too late to plant their corn seed. They want to trade with us for food to keep them during the cold moons." I want to tell him that I have brought Tom to my father, but I dare not say it.

"Ignorant fools!" Manchese raises his voice above the rustling leaves. "Nadie will tell you that you are uninvited guests. We shall treat you with hospitality, according to our custom. But there is no joy in your coming. We shall feed you tonight. Then you must leave us."

He makes his way back to the fire. Master Cooper retreats to the trees. For a moment, I feel that my father will embrace me. Then Tom springs forward, like a mountain lion, and grasps my hand. My eyes warn him to be silent, but it is too late.

"Tell him, Nadie." He is shouting with impatience. "Tell him that I want to marry you. Tell him that the pale people will not leave this land and there must be peace between us. What better way to peace than marriage between two of its people?" I do not translate his words, but Tom places his other hand over his heart.

My father understands. "Are you still a *keegsquaw*?"

he asks me. And it shames me that he should ask such a question, for he knows that it is not our custom to lie with a man before marriage.

"I have honored our custom, father. I want you to welcome Tom and give your permission for me to marry him."

"So, your people have not come before your heart!" His voice falters for the first time. "Then why have you come back, daughter, if you are to leave us so soon?"

"I shall not be far from you," I tell him, "and I must honor my mother's grave."

"So, daughter, you remember your mother at last." His laugh chills my blood as he towers over Tom. "Your metal doesn't make you a man," he shouts. I whisper the words to Tom, ashamed. "Look at the men of Secota. They can kill a bear with their hands. They can wrestle a crocodile to the death. They can track a deer for days without food or water." He pauses, waiting for Tom to reply. But he stands silent, although his grip tightens, taking the blood from my hand. "You come here begging for food. Have you *no* pride? Shall I put you to the breast of a suckling mother? You're a fool, and those with you are fools, too. Why did you come to this land too late to plant your crops?" My father's laughter reaches the treetops, and I bite my lip. "Yes, look at him. With his brown skin, he imagines he's one of us. But he can't see his own eyes, how they flash green like a snake, whose tongue hisses. He does not even bother to pluck the hairs from his face. Go back to where you came from. Go back and suck your mother's milk, *boy*." He says the last word in English.

My heart is hammering because I have never seen my father so angry.

Tom releases my hand. "You can have everything I have, sir...my hammer, my nails, my anvil...whatever you want, if I can marry Nadie."

"What do I want with these things?" My father glances over his shoulder. "Look at the cooking pot your people left last year. It no longer holds *succotash*. It lies full of holes. We can gather clay in the river and make new ones every day." He steps closer to Tom. "I do not want your things. I want what you cannot give me – a husband for Nadie who has Secotan blood running through his body. My daughter is not for you."

He carries on speaking, but I am weeping so much that I cannot explain his words. "She is free to go with you. She is not a prisoner."

I speak my reply in both tongues, but I do not know where I found the courage to say the words. They do not sound real. "Then I shall go with Tom and marry according to his custom."

"If you leave, you cannot come back."

I look past my father's scornful face, to my house with its newly barked roof, to my people, whom I shall give up for Tom. I can no longer imagine a life without him. "I know that," I whisper in my tongue. "Now I must honor my mother's grave."

My father whistles. Amitola appears in the doorway of our house. I would not have recognized her, for she carries a baby on her back and her face is no longer that of a young girl. It is troubled, and I wonder why. Before I can greet her, she disappears into the house.

"We named the child little Nadie," my father says, his voice soft, "for I feared you might not return to us."

My friend and my father! It did not take long. Before I can reply, Amitola emerges with Seekanauk's mother and two young girls, who lift a reed stretcher down the steps. Then they drag it toward me. There is a howling like the wind that brings snow. I do not understand what it is, but fear makes me close my eyes, afraid of what I might see, until fingers claw at my arm, and I open them.

It is my mother – alive.

She is half-sitting, half-lying, her neck twisted. Her skin puckers in angry scars around her neck, along her cheeks and across her eyes. I squat next to her. In the evening light, she smiles as she feels my fringe, frowns as she touches my bare ears and my tears as they spill. Her breath rasps like the air in the forge bellows as she says my name. Her sightless eyes weep.

"Come," my father shouts in English, and I see them from the corner of my eyes, Will and Mary and the others, shuffling forward, circling, eyes wide with horror, Mary turning Joshua's head away.

Seeing my mother thus, I remember my anger for the pale people once more. My father was right. I curse myself. How thoughtless I have been! So lost in my love.

It is not their fault! It is not their fault!

My heart hammers to the rhythm of the words.

I hear Joshua crying because his mother is crying.

I hear Tom's cry catch in his throat, and I wish that my mother could see the bright green of his eyes, the startling yellow of his hair.

"She cannot see your fancy dress," my father says, "but she can hear how you now stumble over your own tongue." He pulls me to my feet, whispering, "The hope of seeing you again has kept her alive. So, daughter, will you stay and be with your mother until she passes from this world?"

Tom and I keep our eyes locked, until this world dissolves as we remember the dark lane, the moonlight sparkling on spiders' webs.

His eyes give their consent, and, in the nod of my head, I agree to part from Tom. Amitola wraps me in her arms, and we weep for all of us, changed by the fire that day.

Tom

I wish I hadn't come. I wish I was in Plymouth, safe in my little forge.

The sight of Nadie's mother sickens me. I've worked with fire all my life, and I've never seen such horror. My father always warned me what it could do, and I've scarcely burned the tips of my fingers.

Her father's the very devil, his chest striped red and yellow, his black hair spiked with feathers. He's played with Nadie, like a lion playing with its prey, as her punishment. Why did he choose to humiliate us before she saw her mother? But he's no worse than my mother. Unhappiness has made them both bitter. Fire leaps in my blood. I want to flatten him like the metal on the anvil.

Nadie tries to beat her breast, as she did that day in the orchard of the vicarage, but she hasn't the strength. Her cry of anguish hardly leaves her lips.

We sit among the trees, watching the sun set over the creek. Only Mistress Payne's tongue lashes. "So we've come on a fool's errand," she says.

The young Secotan men build up the fire until it's taller than a man, and it crackles with summer-dry wood. Then they move back, allowing the older men, draped in wolfskins, to squat close. The wise man leaps to his feet, opens the pouch at his waist and sprinkles powder onto the flames. Sparks shoot into the sky: blue, orange and yellow. Tobacco scents the air. I recognize it from Plymouth quay. He sniffs some of the tobacco, stamps the ground, stares at the sky and calls out strange words. Then he squats again and looks into the flames.

Five women circle Nadie as they escort her to the

fire. I see the glint of Jack's knife. My hand reaches for my own.

"Fine settlers we'd be," Will says, "killing our way out of trouble. You heard what Nadie said. They're peaceful people. They won't harm us, or her."

"Well said, Master Lucas," the Assistant says. "And the rules of England still hold. We came here to settle, not to kill.'

"And to trade," Jack interrupts. "Why don't we offer them our cart for their copper?"

Their chatter sets my teeth on edge. "And what good will copper be to us?" I ask, nodding toward the forest. "That's where we'll be headed in the morning, without Nadie. Copper won't carry your boxes for you."

I look back to their fire. Silence has come to Secota again, except for Nadie's gasp as the women rip off her dress and shift and clothe her in a deerskin skirt. They loop bone and beads around her neck, pierce her ears and put back copper earrings. Her father stands in front of her.

"Now, daughter of Secota, it is time to leave your other world behind." He hurls her clothes into the fire, and they catch at once, bursting into flames. Fragments of charred cloth rain down in the smoke. And, at the smell of the scorching, Nadie's mother runs her hands over her face, trying to smother invisible flames.

It's a pitiful sight.

Then the women drop stones into the flames. On them, they place corn, piled high, and they bring it to us, glistening purple. When we've eaten, the Assistant leads us in prayer. Nadie's people still talk around the fire, but, one by one, we fall asleep, exhausted.

It's still dark when I wake up. Soon, spiders' webs shine their silver in the growing light. As the sun shows through the trees, they come from the house: Nadie and her father. It's strange to see Nadie stooping with sorrow for what's happened, for what will happen today.

"We're not welcome here, Tom," Will calls. "We must look to ourselves." He picks up the rope and tries to turn the cart around. Nadie, tears spilling down her cheeks, remembers our marriage chest, and asks us to leave it; but her father shakes his head.

The cartwheels slither in the mud as Will leans to push with his shoulder. I take my place with him.

I walk with them a little way.

I never expected to part in my own land, only in Plymouth.

Why did I not allow myself to be baptized? Why did I not marry him before we came? How little I have shown my love for him when he came all this way for me.

"Where can we go?" Master Cooper asks me. "We shall not go back to the others with our tail between our legs. We do not need much – some shelter for the winter."

I search my mind. "There is a deserted village by the Roanoke River...two or three days' walk toward the sunrise. It is called Moratoc. It is where your Captain Lane went."

"Deserted?"

"Many people died from the spotted sickness your people brought. They thought it was unlucky to stay."

Tom lets go of the cart and comes to embrace me. "You may as well be across the ocean," he whispers.

"I shall come to you."

"*When?*"

"How can I know that?" I push him away, and he picks up the cart handle again. Mary and Will and Joshua embrace me. Mistress Payne pats my arm. Master Cooper says that he will pray for my mother, ask God to release her from her pain.

My father is not far behind me, shouting after them, and I am glad they will not understand what he is saying. "How do we know that you pale people will not spread everywhere and choke us like the forest vines?

We have to burn *them* to keep our land free."

Eyes linger their last look. Tom...his hair, the color of hickory leaves, flashing as he enters a forest that will be darker than a starless sky, darker than death.

Tom

My heart's sinking. I'd have fought fist to fist for Nadie. Now I've got to wait for her. I try not to think it, wait for her mother to die.

Darkness encloses us. The rain clouds thicken all morning until they burst. At first, we dance like demons, washing our hair and faces and clothes, gasping at the shock of the cold. Everything glistens. There's no gray stone to dull its effect. Then the strength of the rain tears the leaves away, makes a mud so heavy that our ankles ache.

Dips and hollows delay us. We curse and sweat to push that cart along. Light-headed from hunger, I see horses running in front of me, stopping to take our burden from us. Then they dissolve in the unforgiving rain.

My eyes roam over our new colony. Gray strands streak Mary's curls. The strain shows clearly on Will's face. How he's aged. His shoulders have sagged, his knuckles have swollen.

Rose and Henry Chapman, the oldest of us, never falter. Eyes fixed ahead, they support each other through every scratch and stumble, sitting back to back when we rest. In my innocence, I think Jack and Edward will be my friends. After all, they're tin miners. But, like the hammer and the anvil, they can't be apart for long. Joshua, free from his fever, crams his pockets with acorns. Only Agnes and Joyce Payne grumble.

We huddle around the cart at nightfall.

"This is how it must have been in the olden days, when men lived in the forests," the goldsmith whispers. "Since then, we've built beautiful palaces and painted and written books. What makes a man give it all up to live like this?"

"To civilize other people," the Assistant says. "This is how we were before the Romans came to Britain. But for them—"

"We've heard all that before," I interrupt. "Why don't you two just say it? You're scared out of your wits like the rest of us."

We're already slowing down on the second day. Even the fear of another night in the forest can't quicken our pace. Mary and Joyce lead us in singing, but there's no joy in our voices. Each of us misses the words as we think of home with a faraway look in our eyes. We hardly see the sun, sometimes a pale circle when the clouds part briefly. And always that dank smell catching at the back of our throats.

"Don't slow down!" I shout. "We've got to keep going."

"Don't tell me what to do just because you're in love with one of them," Joyce Payne grumbles. "What does she see in you? She could have the pick of any of her men. Her father was right. You're just a *boy*."

The word wounds me, as it did in Secota. Why should Nadie want me? Her men are tall and strong. I can't forget how I last saw her – breasts high, skin glistening, the copper glinting again at her ears.

I curse under my breath.

Long before noon, the clerk, the goldsmith and his family decide to return to Roanoke. The Assistant can't stop them, although he levels his musket and threatens to shoot them for desertion. They leave anyway. Agnes begs to go with them, but Will shakes his head.

"We came all this way for you," he says.

Now I realize. The curve of Agnes's belly when she stretches. As we've grown thinner, she's stayed plump.

"You didn't tell me Agnes was with child."

Will shrugs. "What difference does it make? She's still got to bear the shame." His voice is bitter. "Just when things were going well for me and Mary in Bideford. I was earning good money fitting out ships for Sir Walter. It was Mary who found out...her sister was making a fool of herself with a man already wed. She caused a scandal...but we didn't know she was with child when we left. Thank God we got away!"

He guesses my thoughts. "She's strong and healthy, Tom, but I trust you've helped birth many a foal."

We give little thought to those who've turned back, too concerned with our own worries. It's Master Cooper who misses them. Now, forced into our company, he's haughty. He never tried to befriend us as he did them, and for that, we never forgive him. Only Mistress Payne, who respects authority, is prepared to try. But she quickly gives up, rejected, and from then on, he feels the lash of her tongue like the rest of us.

On the third day, the tree canopy thins and a dull light filters down. The River Roanoke snakes to our right, iron gray in the rain. It's easy to find Moratoc, close to its banks. It's smaller than Secota, only four houses and, like Fort Lane, creepers and vines are choking them. One house – bigger than the rest – is protected by a clump of pine trees – and we set to work at once to repair the roof. We know that just to go through the doorway, just to glance at the horseshoe nailed above it, will give us courage. I pause only to light the fire as dusk creeps upon us. Soon, we're feasting on the corn cakes Amitola gave us, that we've saved for the celebration of our arrival.

We feel strong and brave. We've come through the wilderness alive.

As I let go of Tom's hand, Amitola held up the baby and her warm breath seeped from her rosebud mouth, drying my tears.

I went into the trees at nightfall – our time – and blew kisses into the cooling winds. Some of the children followed me, pursed their lips in mock kisses and ran away when I turned around to scold them.

Now I am lying at my mother's side, like we used to when my father was away hunting, but the pleasure of finding my mother alive is dampened by the pain of parting from Tom. And in my joy at finding her alive, I did not realize how sick she was. During the night, her breath catches, as if the raised scars are snakes squeezing the life out of her. She can barely swallow.

I want her to live, and I want her to die. At the darkest part of the night, when the fire is low and the dogs silent, I cannot believe that she will ever take another breath. Then I am glad she cannot see the anguish in my eyes, for I hardly recognize who she is. I do not mean her puckered skin and unseeing eyes, the twist of her neck. The spirit has gone from her, as surely as the sight has left her eyes. I grieved for her death. Now I must grieve for her life.

Pity softens my anger every time I see her stumble, until I embrace her once more. All that time on the ship, I longed for her to comfort me. Now I let her. Then she asks me what the world is like beyond the horizon. I tell her how the great salt water stretches to another island full of pale people and horses who wear shoes, of their fire that changes the metal, of Hester and Henry. My lips cannot say Tom's name yet, and she does not ask.

The days are busy, for we must prepare for the cold moons. The men hunt, and this brings the biggest shock of all. My father was one of the best hunters in Secota. Now he does not leave the village. He has not left since it burned, Amitola says. He sits with the men too old to hunt.

The hunters bring news as well as the meat that weighs down their shoulders: some of the pale people are moving north on the mainland, others to the island of Croatoan. But there is no news of Moratoc.

We dry fish and strips of meat over the fire. Nuts and grapes shrivel in the noon sun, ready to be stored in earthen pots and buried.

My mother could fashion a pot in the blinking of an eye. Hers were never lopsided, hers never cracked over the fire. Her dishes were always perfectly hollowed. Usually, we decorate our pots only for celebration, but my mother had always decorated every pot she made.

"Daughter, do you remember your father's anger the day he found out?" she whispers.

I nod. My mother hates woman's work as much as I do. As soon as my father went hunting, she used to paint her pots and, because the other women liked her patterns, they exchanged their corn cakes for them. One day, my father took a stray arrow in his leg and limped home in the middle of the day. I remember it clearly… on the steps…my mother leaning over a row of freshly painted pots…biting her lip as she worked, not noticing his shadow fall across her…he cursed, kicked her pots over and trampled on them. He shrieked his shame at her, having a wife who took no pride in woman's work.

Now she must mold and paint her pots with my fingers. My movements are too slow and I smudge the spirals, and I have to clean the clay and begin again. She feels the pattern afterward. "Yes, you are your mother's daughter. Now your hand is steady, your fingers firm."

I tell her of the silver shoes I have shaped for horses, and a smile comes to her lips. Still she does not ask about Tom, and still I do not speak of him. But, sometimes, I change the colors. When my mother tells me to choose blue – for sky and sadness – I take green. When she chooses white – for death and snow – I take yellow.

Tom's colors.

In my mind, I paint his face as Master White painted mine. For the first time, I realize the power of a painting as I came to realize the power of written words. They are our memories. And I am glad that I did not burn Master White's portrait of me in the fire that winter's day.

Amitola has warned me. When I called Tom's name to the trees that first night, the elders thought I was communicating with evil spirits across the water, spirits who would bring back trouble to Secota.

I do not go into the trees again.

I am a pea that no longer fits the pod. Many of my people still fear me, I can see that, and I am glad that my mother cannot. They do not want me to touch their meat or fish, or their children.

Now the dark brings deep sorrow to my heart. Will I ever smile again? As we circle the fire, nobody asks me for my stories. I want to tell them what I have told my mother, but they will not ask me about that part of my life because now it carries shame for my father.

But their silence does not erase the pictures in my mind: the stallion pawing the ground outside the forge;

the ribbon man; Hester reading in the candlelight, her curls falling over her forehead, and I hope that she pauses to think of me.

When my people sing, I cannot sing with them for, to sing, you must be happy and my heart is still like a stone, hardened against the tears that will not stop if I allow them to come. And my people mistake this for dislike of them.

I am no longer one of them. I am standing between the old world and the new. *Popogusso* is not the forge where I first met Tom – it is among my people.

In my mind, I see the others at Moratoc. What is the difference in the lives we lead? We all want the same: fire, food and friendship. What keeps people apart is only the behavior of a few. *There are bad apples in every barrel,* Master White said.

My father is as far away from me as he was when I was in Plymouth. He will not warm toward me.

My mother tries to take my pain away. "That day you were taken, Nadie, he took out his canoe as soon as he returned. He was not afraid of them, or their shooting sticks. He watched for your return every day, as if his heart had been wrenched from his body, although he was still breathing. He married Amitola so that she would care for me as you would have done."

The fire roars with tobacco powder, drowning her whispers. Then I see Tom's face in the very heart of the flames, hear his voice in the hissing pinewood and feel his hands in the smoke that clings to me.

And I smile.

Tom

"God bless our little colony." The Assistant makes the sign of the cross as he speaks. "We must not forget that it is still part of England and we obey the same rules as on Roanoke. Our rations will be the same: two onions a day, some salted beef and biscuits and apples."

"We won't starve," I say, suddenly brave. "There's still fish to be caught. And the forest's teeming with deer and wild pigs and turkeys…"

“And bears and wolves,” Agnes says.

“All food found and killed is to be shared,” Master Cooper finishes.

Only darkness brings back our fear. I volunteer to guard the fire, for I trust nobody to keep it as I can. As my eyelids droop, a hand slips into mine. I think it’s Joshua and I move to take him back to Mary.

But it’s Agnes.

She laughs and entwines her legs with mine, pushing her body against me.

“What are you doing, Aggie?”

“Bringing some pleasure into our lonely lives.”

“Go to Jack and Edward. Two for the price of one!”

She kisses me and, to my shame, my body responds, although my mind does not. “That’s better,” she whispers. She pulls me closer, feeling along my breeches; but I stop her. “It’s safe. I’m already with child. Don’t pretend you haven’t wondered what it would be like with somebody of your own kind.”

“I’ve never lain with Nadie.”

“Perhaps your little Indian is cleverer than I thought.”

She sighs. "I was a fool. Of course, he promised to marry me." To my relief, she lies still.

I can't be angry with her, for she's so much to bear alone.

"Don't you wonder what it would be like?" she asks again.

"Hold your tongue, Agnes!"

She starts to cry, and I stroke her cheek and put my hand on her belly where the child kicks under my fingertips.

"For this I've been forced to come to a new world," she says.

The women make the river work for them. Mary and Mistress Chapman weave a fishing weir as Nadie showed them, although the reeds here seem strong and resistant. Joshua catches frogs with his lobster tail. The men hunt. But the deer always dart away from us. We're too slow, too noisy. So we settle for the small stuff: rabbits, hares, and other creatures we don't recognize.

Our eyes say it instead of our tongues: if we're to

survive, we must live like Nadie's people, not like newly-arrived settlers depending on their supplies. That time on Roanoke hardly counted. This is life in the raw. Sink or swim. Now I miss the palisade of Fort Lane.

The days are darkening early and bringing frost at nightfall, and the harvest moon's waning. After sunset, Will carves a cradle and a wooden horse for Joshua, and I rim its wheels with metal. We all fashion arrows. How I miss the ring of the anvil. Now I make do with a tree stump, but I hate its dull thud. It doesn't make my heart sing. And when I'm making and mending, I imagine Nadie's gentle eyes watching me, her face full of pride.

Agnes often comes to me in the night. I feel her fear and hold her, learning to dampen the lust that rises in me. She, no doubt, pretends that I'm the man who left her with child. If the others find our behavior improper, they never say it, not even the Assistant. I think they pity Agnes now. They see the fear flare in her eyes everyday.

* * *

You can see that John Payne should have stayed in Devon until the day he died. His eyes already have that faraway look I saw in many on Roanoke Island when the *Lion* sailed back to England – always staring beyond the land. Just as the mind sees water on the land, they hope to see land on the water: their England, its fleeting shadows within their grasp for a second. Then it disappears, and their lips tremble. His eyes are as clouded as the November sun. His wife knows that he's slipping away from her and only her lashing tongue rouses him to work.

I ask him why they've come to Virginia.

"I'm a dreamer, Tom," he tells me. "I've always wanted a farm, a little bit of land that I can call my own, with a fence and a gate. But now I've got to face reality, haven't I? And you can't get much more real than this. I'm watching our dream disappear with every pang of hunger, with every insect bite." He stops. "I reckon I've said enough."

Jack and Edward search for copper ore along the

riverbanks. Their father owned a tin mine in Cornwall and has paid heavily for them to come here because his mine's run dry. Anything that glitters seduces them. Envy fills me. They live and work as one, each watching out for the other. This is how brotherhood could be.

But they come back at dusk exhausted, expecting to be fed. "We don't need copper, we need food," Mistress Chapman complains.

Jack, disappointed, grasped my arm one evening. "Did Nadie tell you where the copper was?"

I shook my head.

"Didn't you ask?"

"You don't think we talked about copper, do you?" I scoffed.

"Why not? It's every smith's dream. We can go halves, Tom. We find it. You make it pretty."

"He's not here for the copper, Jack," Agnes cut in, her voice quarrelsome. "He's here for Nadie, his exotic Virginian flower. She thought he was a magic man, not a tinpot blacksmith with hardly two pennies to rub together. If she must take one of *our* men, why doesn't she choose one who can raise her from the dirt, give her silks and shoes and real jewels. She's a savage."

Master Cooper stared at her, his lips pinched. "You are mistaken in that word. The word 'savage' comes from the Latin *silva,* meaning forest. It means simply a man who lives in a forest, nothing more. He is not to be feared. He is governed by natural laws, not ours. He is pure and simple and innocent. Like we were before the Romans civilized us. We shall civilize them in due course, and they will be grateful to us. But I did not come here for the people," he continues, "I came here for Her Most Gracious Majesty, so that she can fight off the Spanish devils."

Agnes fell silent.

And so we pass the autumn, watching the shadows on the horizon. That's what I hate. Not knowing what lies beyond. In Plymouth, I knew: to the north, Dartmoor and the sea beyond Dartmoor; to the west, Cornwall; to the east, the counties stretching to London.

When the long shadows fall over the river and the moaning wind breaks the stillness, I want to howl with the wolves. I'm a dreamer, like John Payne, like Walter Raleigh. And like a dream, Nadie's face is fading.

She's only three days' walk away, but she could be in another world.

Does she *really* exist?

On the seventeenth day of November, we celebrate the accession of Queen Elizabeth to the throne of England twenty-nine years ago. The women have been sewing until last light for days, and we've hunted hard for the hare boiling in the pot.

As dusk falls, we circle the doorway of the big house with fire torches. Then we huddle on logs within them, except for Master Cooper, who refuses to sit with us.

A woman appears in the doorway, white-faced, red-haired and glittering. We leap to our feet and Agnes curtsies as low as her belly allows. The Virgin Queen – in Virginia at last. Only when she comes closer do we see that it's Jack, his face smeared with wood ash, his hair a clump of maple leaves. Silver fish heads decorate his ears and hair, and his lips are purple with grape juice.

Edward scampers to the Queen's side. He glitters as brightly as she does, except for a turkey feather bobbing in his cap. He's curled his hair and mustache, darkened his complexion. He bows low.

"There is a puddle at my feet, Sir Walter," the Queen says. "Take off your cloak."

"Perhaps Your Grace…" Edward makes full use of his Cornish lilt. "Perhaps Your Grace should have used the privy before…"

We laugh until our ribs ache, but the Assistant's face darkens.

"I do not want you to go to Virginia, Walter. It is too dangerous over there."

"But, Your Grace, I cannot send settlers if I am not seen to support them."

"NO, Sir Walter. Your place is by *my* side. I cannot risk losing you."

"What if we lose *them*, Your Grace?"

"There are plenty more where they came from. There are too many people in my country these days. Now lay down your cloak so that I may pass."

Mary wipes the tears from her face. The Assistant stands in front of us. "Stop this foolery," he shouts. "It is treason."

"Then chop off our heads, sir," Will shouts back. "Tom can sharpen my ax for you."

But the spell's broken. We sit, lost in our thoughts, until Joshua sways toward us, hand on his heart, his face, body, arms and legs smeared with river mud. Blue dots ring his neck and upper arms. Acorns swing at his ears. He walks almost on tiptoe, speaking in a lilting rhythm. Then he begins to dance. I laugh. Then, relieved, everybody laughs with me. I know that, in his own way, Joshua's making me think of happier times to come.

The hunter's moon rises like a ball above us. We chatter long into the night, unwilling to go to bed, unwilling to let the fear creep back into our restless sleep.

A fog falls the next morning. It's a light mist at first, which thickens all day until we can't see the river's edge or each other.

No sun. All is shadow.

I break the most important rule: I hunt alone, like poor George Howe, who was killed in the reeds, for I'm sure that the fog will protect me. Winter's brought geese to the river, and I taste them as I track. White flashes in the drab light, and I think the geese have come out of hiding, until somebody's standing in my path, formless at first – and menacing. Then, the shape becomes a young man, cheeks and chest splashed white, and hair bright with feathers. He's taller than me and his broad shoulders hold a bag of arrows and a bow. I call out a greeting in Nadie's tongue, but he shouts words I don't know – harsh sounds like those of a dying man, low in the throat. Sometimes his tongue clicks against his front teeth.

I daren't run. My eyes are fixed on the arrows at his hip. I finger the knife at my waist.

If he'd thrown himself at me or pulled out an arrow, I'd have taken my knife to him. But he doesn't move. Only his eyes roll with contempt. And I see myself as he sees me: tangled hair and beard, skinny, and breeches already tattered.

I'm not worth the fight.

Nadie's father shamed me. But I didn't expect to be shamed by a boy of my own age. He laughs and melts into the fog. I run all the way to Moratoc. It's only the telling and the retelling that takes away my shame: how the Indian was at least seven feet tall, how I held my knife to his throat until he fell at my knees, begging me not to kill him. Agnes listens to my boastings, egging me on.

And I enjoy it.

But Agnes never goes into the trees again. She relieves herself only in a bucket, with a blanket held around her. Will has to empty it, wrinkling his nose in disgust.

It's a far cry from the City of Raleigh.

Doubts always come with the dark, and I seek Nadie's face in the flames.

Sickness has come to Secota.

More than twenty of my people have cheeks and chests spotted red, and eyes watering in the light. Never have we made so many fires to sweat out evil spirits.

Dread fills us once more, for this happened when the pale people first came, when Seekanauk's sister and father died, when many of us – my father and mother, and Amitola – were sick but got better.

It is a time of watching, of waiting.

I feel again the pain of the blisters, the prickling of sore eyes. I thought I would die then. Now my cheeks burn with guilt as I remember the redness of Joshua's cheeks, his fever as we came here.

Those of us who were sick the last time keep well, and we are the ones who tend the others. The sickness tries to take little Nadie from us, but when the death wail is already on our lips, her forehead cools and she smiles.

Two men, four women and five of our children pass into the next world.

"This is what the pale people have brought us!" Manchese cries. "They did not kill us with their shooting sticks. NO. They kill us with their invisible bullets, which lodge in our bodies before we know it and cause pestilence to live in us."

As the wind freshens, the sickness fades. But just as we prepare our celebration fire, our wise man is afflicted, and I wonder if he can foretell his own future, for he screams from the first, as if he can see death's face. His sickness is short. So many spots redden his body that the healer can barely find space to let his blood which he believes contains the invisible bullets; so many spots there is not enough tobacco juice to take away the pain.

This time, our death wail pierces the fog.

The elder women's work begins at once. I cannot remember such a thing, for only important people are placed in the dead house at the edge of Secota, and none of them has died since I was born. The wise man's body is carried to a forest clearing. We cannot watch this secret work, but we all know what is happening. The women pull back the skin and cut out the flesh inside, which is hung over a fire to dry. Like the smell of the fire on my mother's body, like the pig's heart hanging over the forge – it sickens me. When the skeleton has been wrapped in softest deerskins, the human skin is stitched back.

They work quickly, the women who do this work, and, at last, we are invited to join in the feast for the dead. The wise man's body is placed on top of the others lying in the dead house – all chiefs and healers and wise men – all shielded from the sun by reed mats.

At last, we light a celebration fire for the passing of the sickness. Some of us are scarred in mind, some of us in body, and I feel again the sorrow I have brought to my people.

My father sits silent. He must bear the shame and beg forgiveness. He was right. I should not have brought the pale people here.

Tom

Why did we not prepare for winter? We should have dried fish and berries and rationed our beef.

The salted beef has long been used up, although we've still got onions and a few apples. The Assistant's reduced our rations: wheat – and worms – boiled in water, and half an onion a day. And whatever we can catch, which is very little.

We're craftsmen, not hunters.

Hunger haunts us more than our fear of Indians,

bears or wolves. The Assistant's out of his depth. I saw that on Roanoke. He babbles aloud what he writes: "Virginia will be the making of the Virgin Queen. We shall export pitch from the pine trees and wood for her ships."

"Leave off your writing, sir," Will says, "and pull your weight with the work."

"You insult me, Master Lucas. I have not taken more than my fair share of food or water. I have collected firewood."

"You're not part of us, sir," I cut in. "You don't think of the colony anymore, only of yourself. You eat more than the rest of us. And if your mouth isn't full of food, it's full of tobacco."

He sneers. "You sound just like Nadie's father. What are you doing here with *us*? But for you and her, we should all be safe. Now we are at the mercy of this terrible land. They have tamed it. We are trapped by it." He scoffs. "I thought she would have come to us by now. How long can it take for her mother to die?"

My anger flares. I punch him. He punches me back. We come together at last, struggling until we fall to the ground. We slither in the mud. Then we both lie back, too weak to fight. But exhaustion does not stop his tongue.

He staggers to his feet and looks down on me. "Do her people look human with their flat faces and fat noses? Did God really make such creatures? Did—?"

He stops himself, surprised by his own words. Now we all know the ugliness that lies in him, like the worm that burrows into an apple. We only find it when we bite deep.

It's too late. I pull him back to the ground, hammering blows on his body. I would have stamped on his head if Will hadn't stopped me. Then I sit by the fire to dry my clothes, grudgingly making room for him to do the same, our precious energy wasted in anger.

I want everybody to see the beauty I see in Nadie – her gleaming skin and hair, her beautiful eyes, and the gracefulness of her walk. Will there always be white people who shrink from her? I saw it on the faces of Walter and Abigail – and my mother.

There was little satisfaction in the fight. Anger destroys, as rust destroys metal.

I saw it in myself after my father had died, after Francis had left for Tavistock. It had been a day of such heat, so stifling that I'd almost let the fire go out. A few embers glowed. My mother was unsteady with ale. "Why didn't *you* go?" she jibed. "I don't want to look at your yellow hair day in, day out." She threw her ale at the wall, splattering the plaster. Then she thought I was him – my father – and she hung her arms around my neck. "Kiss me, John. You *never* kiss me." She fell back onto the bed, still clutching me. Disgust filled me. I slapped her face. It stopped her in her tracks. She cried a little, then she fell asleep.

From that day, I curbed my anger. Now I'll curb it again. I'll take my example from Will. He never wanted to come here. He made the sacrifice for his sister-in-law, to save her shame. He longs for Devon.

Agnes's baby slips into our little world without fuss on a frosty night, bruised and faintly blue, with a soft mewl that rises to a piercing cry. "Now we're thirteen," she whispers. And with him, joy comes briefly into our lives. Joshua welcomes his cousin with kisses and laughter.

We hunt all that Christmastide Eve and return empty-handed. Joshua puts a circle of rope in front of a silver birch, places his precious acorns inside and waits until two turkeys peck the frosting acorns. Then he tightens his rope, catching one by the legs. We feast together in the big house, among pine cones and branches and candles spitting turkey fat. We sing. Joshua pulls his wooden horse. Then we fall silent, listening to baby Joseph snuffling in his milky sleep and think of the people we've left behind…

I remember that night, on the tower of Saint Andrew's church, with the stars all around us, the warmth of Nadie's neck in the chilly air, the way she leaned back against me...not meeting my mother's eyes when we reached the ground…

"We survived on the *Lion,*" Mary says, "in that terrible fog near the Caribbean Islands. We knew then we had to sight land to be safe. Now we've got to sight spring."

"Think of what we are trying to do," Mistress Payne says. "We're the first of our people to put down roots in this new world. God gave us the earth to explore. We're pioneers. We shall *own* land, given time, something we can only dream of in England, where it is handed only to the rich. Here we've got a chance."

"If we live long enough," Will replies.

The frost comes the day after Christmas. Icicles sparkle on dead stalks, trembling in the early sun, before they freeze again. A small bird, its fluttering captured in a frozen moment, perches in death. For a few days, we're taken into a magical world, a world of wonder, and we don't realize how hungry we are, how lost we are.

The last light flickers in Rose Chapman. She dies in her sleep, without a sound. Henry refuses to leave her grave. We build a fire next to him, wrap him in our blankets, but he gives up. He's dead by the new year. We miss them. They were gentle people – too gentle for this land.

My people forgive easily. Only my father does not. Now that the sickness has left us, I sense a change. Amitola says it is because I have been dutiful and cared for my people. Some of them think that the pale people have used me to bring the sickness, so that they can replace our people when they die.

I would once have laughed at such a thought, knowing the kindness of the ones who brought me here; but since Master White's morning raid on

Desamonquepeuc, I am not so sure.

How will Tom bear the cold in Moratoc? In Secota, close to the great salt water, the snow does not crust, and the cold does not bite through our bearskins.

If only I had gone with them for a short time to show them how to survive. But how could I? I had to stay to care for my mother, to soften a father whose face sharpens when he looks at me.

Does he think I shall change my mind and stay in Secota?

Amitola looks away when I ask her. And my mother has nothing to say. I wish she was not blind because then I could look deep into her eyes and see what she was thinking. But the puckered flesh tells me nothing.

It *is* easy to be lulled by my old life. Sometimes, when my mother is calm and sleeping, when I hear my father's laugh as he smokes by the fire, I can forget what has happened, until I remember that my portrait hangs on the vicarage wall. Was I ever really there? Was it not just a painting that Master White took back with him? Then the fire hisses, bringing back Tom in flesh and blood.

I must wait, as I waited in Plymouth. I shall be patient,

for I am meant to be with him. Why else did my guiding spirit take me to him?

Last night – the longest night of the year – Seekanauk walked me away from the fire, to the trees where the darkness was thick, and pulled me to him, expecting me to rest my head against his bony chest. So I did. But I pushed my fist into my mouth so that I would not laugh. Then he cupped my face and leaned over to kiss me. I struggled free and turned away so that he kissed my ear, whilst his hand touched my breasts.

I could not help it. I laughed. Then he laughed, too, curved his arm around my shoulders and we stood, friends again, watching the birds settle into sleep, the sun redden. And when I went back to the fire, my father was smiling at me for the first time.

I *laughed*.

How long is it since I heard that sound? It brings me Tom in Back Lane, touching my tangled hair.

Amitola kept a place for me by the fire, and I sang with her. Inside, I was weeping.

Tom

God played a trick on us. Bellies full from turkey succotash, hope restored, we let down our guard. We huddled around the fire after Christmastide, talking of our return to Roanoke, tasting the food the supply ship would bring. Tomorrow, we'll hunt, we promised. We didn't see the swollen sky, didn't hear the wind whipping in from the east, so lost were we in our future.

"Smells like snow," I said.

"Smells like tobacco," Jack replied. Then he went

outside, although Edward tried to stop him. "I'll not pee in a pot in this godforsaken land," he said.

How blind we were.

Hour after hour, the wind howls its rage, rattling the roof, lifting layers of bark. It screeches like a thousand wolves, worse than any sea squall. When we look through the window slits, all is white, like a foaming wave bearing down on us. Jack doesn't come back. We sleep briefly and wake with ice in our hair and eyelashes. Frost laces my beard. Smoke, unable to escape, stings our eyes. The firelight shows what we fear. Snow has smothered the house. I poke a hot iron through the roof and judge it to be about four feet deep. We move like shadows, afraid to disturb the white beast that engulfs us, knowing that we can't look for Jack. Edward weeps for him.

We know when night comes only because the wind and the wolves howl together. Why does this wind never take a breath so that we can hear each other speak?

"It's worse than those first days on the *Lion,*" I shout to Will. "Then we could go up on deck when the air was foul."

"Aye, I've imagined death many times – drowning at sea, snapped up by a wild animal, my neck shattered by an arrow. But I never imagined this."

We're in deep trouble.

Those first few days of snow, we still have onions and all the snow water we need. With turkey bones and Joshua's acorns, the cooking pot keeps away the worst pangs. Edward sits by the window gap, pulling at the frozen reed mats that Will's nailed there. I wrap Jack's blanket around him, but he shakes it off. The anvil's no use without the hammer.

By the second week, we're restless with gnawing hunger and Master Cooper's forced to throw his tobacco leaves into the water. Will finds rats in the roof, frozen as they scurried, but he's forbidden to add them to the pot. So we make a smaller fire to roast them.

Ice is our enemy now – as bright and as sharp as metal. Starvation stalks us, more deadly than any feathered boy in the trees. When our eyes cloud, we think of home: roasting meat, bread fresh from the oven, eggs beaten with warm milk. My lips suck at imagined pastry as I chew the leather of my blacksmith's apron.

Did Nadie warn me how cold the winters were?

I think so. But I was too drunk with love to listen.

Nothing quietens Joseph. Agnes keeps him to her breast all the time; but he draws up his legs and wails. Then he stops. He never cries again. A low whimper, a gasp and little Joseph leaves our world. We avoid Agnes's eyes for we're glad of the peace. She sacrifices her shawl for him and we lay him to rest in the snow outside the window, until we can bury him.

It changes Agnes. She doesn't cry, but her beautiful blue eyes are as hard as the midwinter ice. Her face is ugly with anger, her voice full of bitterness.

"I've been forced to sail halfway across the world because of a man and now I'm stranded," she says. "Was it worth it for you, Tom? Coming all this way for that little...savage. We're no better than wild animals."

I forgive her, for her eyes brim. "We'll be back on Roanoke soon. Imagine, Aggie! The supply ships will bring us apples and cheese and... We can plant crops for next spring."

"Come back to England with me, Tom. I can be like a daughter to your mother. We can start a new life."

"I'm doing that already."

The flames lull me. I think of her breasts, still full and milky. But I push her away.

"Haven't you ever been in love, Agnes?"

I leave her weeping, and Joshua comes to nuzzle her nipple like a newborn.

Everybody's hungry in a different way. Most of us are cold and quiet. Only the Assistant, without his tobacco, paces up and down. Edward's fingers bubble black. I've often seen it in horses with infected hoofs and know the dangers; but he won't let me put the hot iron to them.

We talk only of the supply ship being prepared, its timbers cleaned and sealed with pitch, barrels being filled with biscuits and salted meat, sails being sewn where they've split in the winter storms. We imagine John White smiling because he'll see his granddaughter, see the speckle of her first tooth, see how straight she sits.

And I think only of Nadie as I chip wood from the roof and walls, chop up boxes and chairs – anything to keep the flames alive. We would have fanned it with our last breath. Only the empty cradle remains, for Agnes won't let us touch it.

The last candle dies out. We no longer talk. We haven't the strength. Is it day or night? It doesn't matter much, for we want to sleep like bears.

But the fire matters. We huddle, watching the flames rise and fall. In their flicker, I see Nadie's mouth curve into a kiss. Sometimes, when the flame threatens to go out, I stretch out my hand to gather dust from the floor, and when I scatter it, it sparkles, stealing the stars from my head.

The deerskin should have warned me.

My father brought it to us – the best one from the hunt. Amitola has already tanned it over the fire and removed the hair without cutting the skin. Now it has to be softened, to be made into a deerskin skirt for me. That is our custom. My mother does not want me clothed in the one my aunt gave me, for it is a mother's delight to provide a deerskin skirt for her daughter. I have been taught such work from an early age, but I am not skilled.

I do not have the patience, and I have torn many a skin with a clumsy movement. Now I try harder to please my mother.

This work fills the darkest days of cold and snow. From time to time, Seekanauk's mother comes to watch, though not to help – and she is pleased to see my woman's work.

How dull this work is after the pleasure of painting. It numbs my mind as well as my fingers. But I try to soften the skin with love, for this is what my mother needs now – to have a deerskin skirt for her daughter, so smooth that no puckers chafe her young skin. My arms ache. They did not ache when I hammered the metal. Then Tom was by my side, and my body held the warmth of love. Now, a chill stiffens it all the time.

I feel as if I have withered like the vine leaves that still cling to the bare branches, buffeted by the wind and snow. Everything is dry: my food, my hair, my skin. My father sends my aunt to paint my old tattoos and to massage my skin and hair with sunflower oil.

And still I do not understand.

There are nods of approval as I walk outside, my

beauty acknowledged by all. The crisp air is full of whispers, but I cannot hear them, until the day when the sun has its first strength, when the first corn is sown, and my father shakes Seekanauk's hand and they embrace each other like father and son.

How could I not have seen it? Have I not often seen young girls grind corn, weave baskets and soften deerskins – all to please the mothers of their future husbands? And I thought I was so clever with all my new learning.

Amitola will not tell me what she knows. "Your father commands me to be silent," she says. "What can I do? You must ask him."

I find my father staring into the fire, breathing in tobacco. I kneel in front of him, longing for him to embrace me as he used to, but the look on his face still shuts me out.

"Father, I have been a dutiful daughter, and Amitola has held her tongue. Now I ask you. Am I to marry Seekanauk?" I steady my breath, hoping it is not true, for I want the two of us to be at peace.

He nods.

"But I have promised Tom..." Pain shoots through me, like hot iron on flesh. I wish I had allowed myself to remain ignorant. We are all standing in the shadows – my mother, my father and I. And I know that if I marry Seekanauk now, I can bring us all back into the light.

My father walks away. All these cold moons, a fire has burned inside me, my love for Tom. Now it burns with the cold flame of fear.

There is no surprise on my mother's face when I tell her. She finds the strength to put her arms around me. "Pray to the gods to help you, Nadie, as I do." She holds me tighter.

"But what if Seekanauk insists that..."

"He loves you too much for that," she replies. "He will wait if he has to."

Her words comfort me and I rest against her, letting her protect me as she used to when I was a child.

Tom

God is good.

This morning, we saw the orange glow of the sun through the ice and heard the steady drip of water from the roof. In the brightening light, we saw what hunger had done to us: Mary gaunt and gray; Agnes staring as if dead. And still Master Cooper – like a rattling skeleton – paced up and down, as if he feared that death would claim him if he stayed still, calling out to God. My heart sinks at his babbling, for he sees the light as the light of Heaven and thanks God for taking us in.

The pot bubbles, mocking us with its melted snow, but we drink it to keep our bodies warm.

By noon, the snow's thin enough for us to see the outline of the sun, as pale as the moon in a clear sky. We take it in turns to hollow out the snow – except for Edward – using our hands, for the spade's too heavy to lift. We cry out as the cold burns our fingers. By dusk, we see the trees again, and suck in air so chilled that it makes us cough.

Tomorrow, we hunt.

It turns out that we must hunt Master Cooper instead. I remember seeing him during the night, standing in the doorway, and thought I was dreaming. But he was gone this morning, the outline of his footsteps blurred because he was shuffling along.

Pity fills me. What was it like to walk off alone under such a starry sky? Did he believe he was in Heaven?

Will and I take bows and arrows and lighted branches to search for him. The wilderness dazzles us.

The branches are still crusted with ice. Here and there, where the noon sun's caught the tips, the ice has melted and frozen again, cascading like a frozen waterfall. Animals have disturbed the ground ice, spraying frozen snow into the air, where it hangs against the tree trunks like the lace on Nadie's sleeves.

We follow the Assistant's tracks toward the river, which sparkles against a sharpening horizon. A white wilderness behind us. A white wilderness in front. The ice is gleaming brighter than any metal I've polished. Above us, the sun rises cold red, and the moon wanes. The wind, still baying, forces us to walk on the spot until we break free. It scoffs as we stumble forward, crying out at the cold around our feet. The effort to move leaves us light-headed. There are other tracks, too, and I hesitate, remembering the boy with the bright feathers in his hair.

"Looks like bear prints," Will says.

If we have not caught a bear by midwinter day, we fear for our lives, Nadie said.

Will sees the bear first, dark against the mouth of the cave, awoken from its winter sleep by the early warmth.

Sniffing the air, it lurches toward us. We let it come into the trees, where we circle him. Then we fire our arrows in turn. Some fall with a thud, but some arch well and find their mark in the bear's arms and legs. He raises himself, paws the air, clouds of breath hiding his head. Then he snarls and runs forward, catching Will's cheek with his claws.

"I'll not risk my life," he cries, moving back. Blood lies frozen on his cheek. "I must think of Mary and Joshua."

"You've already risked it by coming to Moratoc," I shout. "This is our last chance, Will."

I stagger toward the bear, singeing his fur with my firebrand, forcing him against a tree. He growls as he climbs, watching us from the lowest branch. It's easy after that. We fire our arrows again. Will, still the strongest of us all, stops him in mid-roar with an arrow through his neck. The bear groans. Then he topples.

I stab hard, high with the kill. The bear gives a last roar, then he slumps forward, his blood melting the snow beneath him. We fall to our knees and thank God. And under my breath, I thank the bear.

One life for another, but both sacred.

A howl comes from the ridge of the cave. Others answer it. Wolves, their appetite aroused, slink toward us. There are at least six of them, ugly brutes bubbling saliva as they howl, bellies brushing the snow. When we wave our flames against their sniffing noses, they back toward the ridge, reluctant to leave us.

We hack. We cut. We slash. We each carry chunks of meat and bearskin, leaving enough to satisfy the wolves. As soon as we move away, they come back, hurling themselves onto the remains, giving us safe passage. We don't talk any longer of searching for Master Cooper because we can only think of filling our bellies.

Happiness fills me.

I've survived in Nadie's land as she survived in mine.

Day after day, icicles soften on the stalks. Frost crackles on the branches. We glimpse green in the forest. Slowly we stretch our limbs and breathe in fresh air. The sunlight's unkind to us. We try not to notice our sores and bleeding gums.

It's been like a long sea voyage – without the sea.

As the sun warms, the river rushes with melting ice. I tie a rope around my waist and wade out to wash. My puny body revolts me: muscles slackened, ribs raised, skin deadly pale. I smell the pine trees, the new green of the birch, the unfolding flowers of the clematis.

It's as intoxicating as ale.

Mary trims my beard and hair. Agnes washes my shirt. I'm a young boy again, preparing to court his love. When will Nadie come to me? I must take care, for when she does she will be weighed down with sorrow at her mother's death.

And in these preparations, we all spring into life like the forest around us. Will and I repair the cart. Joshua polishes the rusty wheel rims. Hardly believing what we're saying, we talk of leaving. We look down the river, shading our eyes, talking as if we can already see the supply ship on the horizon.

The snow melt gives us back little Joseph, his skin ice-blue, his tiny fingers splayed like stars. Agnes weeps, but it's Joyce Payne who cannot be consoled.

"The ground's still too hard to dig. We can't leave

him for the animals," Will says. "We should burn him."

It's the saddest fire I've ever seen. The wet wood smolders. Its flames never leap to Heaven. A plume of dark smoke rises through the trees. The smell sickens us and brings the wolves too close. But we defend Joseph's funeral pyre to the end, placing circles of burning torches around it, and only when his little body's burned to the bone do we think of leaving.

Master Cooper's words haunt me: *How long can it take for her mother to die?*

It's agreed. We can't go straight to Roanoke Island, for Nadie might still come. We'll go to Secota first. But we linger another day…and another. Nobody dares to admit: we're afraid to leave the safety of Moratoc, afraid to enter the wilderness once more. At last, we force ourselves to wrap our few possessions in our blankets, and, thanking God for sparing us, we settle to sleep our last night at Moratoc, watching the moon rise through the rotting roof.

Eight of us. Almost a third of our colony dead or disappeared.

How have the others fared?

And Nadie?

I don't care how I marry her, only that we should marry.

And when I wake suddenly in the night, to the sound of whispering leaves, my first thought is: today, we set off to see Nadie.

Will she still want me?

They come in that half-light, before dawn, the men with bright feathers in their hair, who click with their tongues and lash us with vine ropes. By sunrise, we're already deep in the wilderness, wrists and ankles tied.

Joshua laughs at first, perched high on his father's shoulders, face to face with butterflies and birds. Nobody speaks, except for the feathered men who sound like the chickens at home.

But when the sky darkens, he asks to get down. "I'm tired of this game," he cries.

The snow has melted, but the frost still pinches at dawn and dusk, leaving the earth cleansed and hard underfoot. The days are longer and lighter, and I long to be out of my darkness.

I hear Tom's mother, that day on the quayside, when her face suddenly softened: *There is nothing stronger than first love. It holds you in its grip like ice. But ice gives up its grip when spring comes again.*

Now the wind is gentle, bringing the scent of rising

sap and the song of newly arrived birds. The vines and honeysuckles swell, but my mind darkens.

Will Tom think I have forgotten him? Is he already with Agnes, who walked too close to him as they left? Is he still alive?

As the jasmine leaves thicken and coil around the branches, my throat tightens. When I am planting corn, I watch the path into the trees, longing to leave. Soon, they must go back to Roanoke.

Will they come this way first?

Sometimes, I look up, thinking I can hear the rattle of the cart. But there is only silence, except for the scratching of twigs as we sweep, and the snapping of the last dried corn over the fire.

The women pity me. They whisper as much as they did in Plymouth.

Once, I could have married Seekanauk. I could have sacrificed myself like the man nailed to the tree. But now that I have loved Tom, I cannot.

In the spring sunlight, his face returns to me with such force that it takes my breath away. To my shame, as I listen to my mother's shallow breathing, I pray that each breath will be her last, to release me, for I cannot leave her until she is at peace. Sometimes, the breath is so long coming that I lean over her, put my ear to her lips.

The jasmine flowers bud, as pink as dawn. My father sniffs, like a lion scenting its prey. "Soon you will truly be with your people again, daughter," he repeats. He would have had me married before my mother died, but Seekanauk, knowing my reluctance, does not insist.

The forest stifles me, and I stand on the edge of the creek, where the water swells and splashes.

A splash of water and I could have married Tom.

One evening, when jasmine flowers light the dusk with a scent so strong that I can hardly breathe, my mother strokes my hand. "Nadie," she whispers, "I cannot die while you are here, for I cannot bear to part from you again. Look at me, skin and bone and blind... I do not want to live like this. I want you to go to Tom and let me go to my gods. Then we shall both be happy." She presses into my palm her father's *tinda* pouch – his firelighter – a sharp stone tied to the end of a stick and a copper-lined stone, to make the sparks fly.

This is the greatest gift of all – given to those who must make an important journey.

I try to lie beside her, but she finds the strength to push me away.

And I leave before I can think about what I am doing. I glance back from the doorway. No flames lick my mother's body. She stares after me with unseeing eyes. This time, I leave of my own free will, but I would rather somebody had taken me away, for my feet drag on the ground.

My father is sleeping, his arm around Amitola and the child. I glance at him, fearing that he will open his eyes. But I know that he will not come after me, even if he sees me leave. His pride would not allow it. I shall shame my father a second time, and there will be no coming back for me, whether I find Tom or not.

Once among the trees, my breathing calms.

My people once mourned my leaving. Will they mourn me now that I have deserted them for a pale man?

Tom

I don't remember many of the words of Nadie's tongue. It's difficult enough to speak my own. But I remember one, for it made Nadie laugh when my tongue caught my teeth.

Popogusso.

Twenty days' walk north, through untouched wilderness, brought us to our pit of hell. We saw no villages, no smoke among the trees. We only saw each other's backs as we stumbled, saw Edward and John

Payne tossed aside when they died. We were bent and bowed, like trees in a spring squall.

Our hell's an island where the River Roanoke widens and forks, where the river laps green around its rocks, for this is where the Mangoak extract copper. When I first saw the rising rocks, in my light-headed thoughts, I thought we'd come to Drake's Island, which lies off the coast of Plymouth. My father used to row us there on summer nights, to fish.

How long since we came here? I know exactly. Three weeks and five days. It's almost the end of May and darkness comes late. And since we work every daylight hour, I long for winter.

There are no other white captives, but other dark-skinned people, whose eyes show shock at the sight of us, for they've not seen pale people before. Six of us – two men, three women and a boy – who aren't allowed to speak in our own tongue as we work amongst hissing water and spitting flames, who endure the torments of hell by exchanging smiles and nods and small kindnesses.

Mary, Agnes, Joyce Payne and Joshua must light

the fires in the clefts of the rocks. As the rocks heat, they haul pots of water from the river and empty them over the hot rocks. The water hisses as they split open. When they've examined them for copper ore, they move on to fire other clefts. It's dangerous work. Joshua's fingers are already burned and blistered. Will and I light a fire under the copper-streaked rocks they bring us, the hottest fire I've ever felt. Then the copper runs, dazzling us as the sun catches it. We let it cool. Then we heat it again and again. These are not fires that bring me Nadie's face, but cruel fires that singe my beard and hair, and scorch my skin.

Then the cooling copper must be hammered. The Mangoak prize me and Will because we brought hammers with us. We take pride in our work, even here. We don't miss the metal and break our fingers; but our eyes ache from its sheen.

I'd give anything to work such a metal. These words, the ones I spoke to Nadie on Plymouth quay, torment me, for I've given Nadie.

My guilt grows as Mary's hair turns gray. If I'd not taken Nadie to Secota, we wouldn't have gone to

Moratoc. If we hadn't gone to Moratoc...the thoughts hammer inside my head. I must hold on to the Tom who rushes to shape the metal before it cools, who made horses lift their hoofs at the touch of his hand – the Tom who came to the end of the world for love. The look in Nadie's eyes when I left haunts me.

Now our winter in Moratoc seems like Heaven.

We sleep in shallow caves just above the water, roped in pairs. I'm tied to Mary, Will to Agnes. The Mangoak do this, for they know that captives sometimes pleasure each other to relieve their misery and they watch, faces smirking.

And always, before sleep, my exhausted mind asks: *Has Nadie gone to Moratoc, or to Roanoke?* Then I shake the thought away, otherwise I can't sleep.

Every morning, we realize: we're not just captives who could be set free. We're slaves, who'll be worked to death. Every night, we remake the same promise: nobody must escape, for the others will be punished.

The Mangoak – about a dozen of them – have houses higher on the rock, away from the water, where they can look down on us. There's only one woman with them, her body glowing with copper. She's wary of Agnes when she brings our corn. Her eyes seem to say: One day, you'll replace me.

Agnes is the only one of us allowed to fetch water. The Mangoak favor her, for she never speaks, and they enjoy watching her wash at the water's edge. They nudge each other and laugh.

Who will help us now?

Moratoc is not far for me, for I am sure of the way and fleet-footed. I run in their wheel ruts, weeping for my mother. My heart aches for the journey they made, uncertain and afraid, and with the heavy cart to pull. I find rotted apple cores, one with a seedling sprouting, and rotting corn leaves.

Jasmine tumbles through fresh-leaved trees, its flowers like stars lighting the way. New life teems around me. I stop only to rest and eat but not to sleep. My heart lurches at the thought of seeing Tom. When I hear the rush of the River Roanoke, I stop to smooth my hair, to press jasmine petals against my sweaty skin, bathe my swollen eyes. I call out their names, as we did that day on Roanoke.

My ears wait for the sound of their voices. My eyes long for the first glimpse of Tom. How will he look now? Thin and pale, like Francis? Will the fire still be in his eyes? Or will the winter wilderness have dulled him? Will they all meet me like ghosts, as thin as winter branches? Will they have survived?

Nobody answers my call.

I was right. It *is* a good place. That is where they must be living, in the big house, newly roofed with bark, set under a cluster of pine trees, a horseshoe hanging over its doorway. Logs are piled outside.

"Tom? Mary?" Wild pigs run from the house, squealing.

Moratoc is not as derelict as Fort Lane, and the vines are only just starting to creep across the roofs. The big house still looks like a family house whose occupants have gone out and stopped to pick berries on the way back – and who will be angry to find that they have let the fire go out.

That is the shock. No fire. No cooking pot.

I poke the fire. There is no red glowing at its heart. I take a deep breath and enter the house. The wind has blown a fine dust everywhere – over mossy beds, benches, the plates and spoons still set out. My stomach turns over, for the air is sour and reeks of despair. Clothes spill from loosely tied blankets. I recognize Agnes's dress, Mary's linen, my marriage box, its lid still nailed down – and Tom's blanket. I bury my face in it, breathing its damp smell. Then I spread it out in the sun. I do not go back inside, for I cannot bear that smell.

I wait until dusk, but nobody comes. The sky darkens, but I am afraid to light a fire. At last, I sleep, wrapped in his blanket, thinking: They *must* be coming back. If they had already left for Roanoke, they would have taken the cart.

The morning sky is a brilliant blue. I do the tasks I dislike: sweeping and scouring the cooking pot. When I force myself to enter the house again, I find wrinkled acorns, a wooden toy horse, already green with mold, the torn pages of a book and tufts of bearskin. My heart lifts.

If they have killed a bear…

I imagine that Tom is out hunting, that our child lies asleep in the wicker cradle at my feet. *Whose* cradle? *Whose* bones lie in the pile of wood ash under the silver birch?

I wait for six nightfalls, lifting my arms to the setting sun, asking the gods to show me what to do. Shall I go on to Roanoke? Or shall I return to my mother, and beg my father's forgiveness? I did not expect to be so afraid. Sometimes, I kneel, my hands clasped, repeating some of Henry's words.

When a voice cries out on the seventh morning, somewhere in the distant forest, it speaks in the English tongue. Relief floods me. They must have moved deeper into the forest for warmth, away from the winter floods, or lost themselves on their way back. I run toward it, toward the hill. I do not recognize the voice that cries, *"Ugly devils…swarming like bees…"* but I recognize that there is madness in it.

A man lurches from the shadows. It is Master Cooper, wearing only a nightshift that hardly covers his knees. His feet are bare, his cheeks scratched scarlet above the matted hair on his face. He cries out as he walks, staring ahead like a man without sight – or like a man who does not wish to see.

I show myself, calling my name, struggling to speak his tongue again. "It is Nadie, sir. You came to my village, to Secota…Tom and I…"

"I saw them…" He looks past me. "…slipping silently into Moratoc, their feathered heads nodding like awakening birds, swarming like bees around the honeypot…ugly little devils, snarling and shouting." He grimaces. "Where is God?"

I soothe him, as I used to soothe Tom's horses. "Are the others with you, Master Cooper?" At the sound of his name, he looks at me. Then he speaks again, spitting out the words. "…Savage with your breasts uncovered, sin in the sight of God, an abomination, devils from the darkness trying to marry into the light, but refusing to come into the light of God's family, devil child…"

"Hush." I grip his arm, trying to sit him on the ground

beside me, but he is too agitated. With movements of madness, he circles and I track him like prey as he hurls his poisonous words… "Baby conceived in sin, born in sin, died in sin…"

"*Whose* baby?"

His eyes stare past me again. Then he sprawls over a log, showing shrunken buttocks.

"Master Cooper, where is Tom?"

As he opens his mouth, they rise from the bushes.

Two Mangoak.

They are everything I have ever feared: chests enclosed with copper; gleaming hair spiked with red and yellow feathers; twisting lips, silent until their tongues click like crickets. They could have already taken my tongue because I cannot speak. They pull the Assistant to his feet and cuff his head.

But he is beyond fear. "Copper! Copperheads!" he spits. "Devils, like you, rejected and unfinished by God, savage, savages!"

"Leave him!" I speak at last in my tongue, tugging the Assistant's arm.

The Mangoak glance at each other. "Come with us,

my little *keegsquaw*," the young one says in my tongue. "Then we'll let him go." His breath fans my cheeks as he touches my earrings. "Such beauty as yours should be covered in copper from top to toe."

"Where are they?" I ask. I turn back to the Assistant. "What did you see, sir?"

A glint of blade. A cry of pain. A gurgle. Then he falls, spurting blood from his mouth. In a second, his tongue is held high. "Go home, child, back to your mother and father and their stories of the terror tree. Go home, before it's your turn," the old one clicks. "Why do they let a child roam alone on our land? I should not allow my daughter to be alone in such a place."

"Where are they?" I whisper.

But they leave without a word, as silently as they came. I would have fainted but for the Assistant, who is clutching my ankles. I staunch his blood with moss and clean his mouth. At last he lies next to me, and I close my eyes.

I sleep late into the morning, for his body blots out the sun, dangling from a tree, hung by his nightshift, like Christ on the cross. And I shudder. For us, hanging is the worst sort of death because it prevents the dead from traveling into the next world.

I climb the tree to let him down. From it, I see what he last saw, the river glinting down to the sea, the village fires glowing in the misty dawn.

And but for the bloodstains on the ground, I would have thought it all a dream. I cover his body with ferns and branches. At nightfall, I set out after the Mangoak, for I have no doubt that they will take me to Tom.

To make a journey when you do not know how, or when, it will end is the most difficult journey of all. But I have done it once before, and it brought me Tom. Sometimes I pass broken twigs, blackened earth from their fires, a feather on the forest floor. They go by day. I go by night.

Only once do I think: If the Mangoak have Tom, what can I do?

Then I have to bury the thought. Otherwise, I cannot go on.

Tom

Four weeks and two days.

We're all losing the little strength we had when we came here, barely recovered from our winter starving. Fingers now numb, not with cold, but bruised by the hammer until I hardly feel the pain. If it were not for the others, I would run while I had enough strength, although the sight of the Mangoak's woman puts the fear of God into me. She ran off last week, into the late dusk, taking our corn, slipping into the water.

She swam without surfacing. I saw her climb onto the bank and run like the wind. But the whistles screeched.

They brought her back in the moonlight as we huddled in the cave, still hungry. She was whimpering, coughing strangely. In the morning, she brought our food, eyes fixed in terror, her blood-crusted lips stiffened into silence.

When I saw what had happened to her, hope drained from me and my strength faded as quickly as the short darkness of summer.

Now I work the metal carelessly, bruising and breaking my fingers until I can't feel them, only feeling the lash of the vine rope across my shoulders.

But, although my body's weakened, my mind's still strong. I've survived the winter for Nadie. Now I must survive this.

If Nadie's come to Moratoc now, she'll go on to Roanoke to fetch Master White. A round of musket balls will free us, and those poor nameless slaves on the other side of the rock. Our eyes search the far bank all the time, watching the clematis tumble, the leaves thicken, the river swell with salmon. We imagine our names called in the wind.

How long can it take for her mother to die?

My mind's restless with thoughts of escape, but Will makes me promise not to try, for the punishment it might bring to those left behind. And so I bide my time, until the worst horror is upon us.

I thought that Agnes would weaken first, but it's Mary who sickens with the flux. Working with the fire hasn't melted the ice in Agnes's eyes, but a hardness deep inside holds her like a metal rod. In her mind, she's somewhere we've never been, and this allows her body to go on working, although her hair whitens and her teeth loosen.

Mary's vomited all night, and flux stains her skirt. She's calling out to God to set her free. The guard lashes her as she staggers at the river's edge. Will wants to snatch the whip from his hands, but Mary's eyes beg him not to.

It's the most terrible day of our lives.

Toward dusk, as we're roped together, she calls out again to God. Mistress Payne takes her hand and sings.

Her voice soars higher than it's ever done. The Mangoak call down from the rocks, anger in their voices. My body tenses as I wait for them to flash their knives in warning, to silence that glorious voice forever. But, to my surprise, they fall silent.

Mary dies with the sunset, but we do not tell our captors, for we want the short night to say our farewell, want one more night with her body unblemished, for we know how her hand will be mutilated in the morning.

That's the greatest cruelty. Even in death, our bodies aren't safe.

We weep long into the summer night, when the sky never really darkens. But hope mingles with my grief, for my escape path's clear to me now. I can't speak it, for the others might call out to me at the last moment. I'm sure that Will understands, for his eyes brighten for a moment. I say farewell in my mind, and close my eyes, hypnotizing myself with thoughts of Nadie.

How do snakes survive? They slither at nightfall and curl under a rock at sunrise. I am that snake. My body becomes my arms and legs. My tongue curls to catch berries and suck the evening dew as I move.

But fear changes the way we see the world. The same wilderness, the same birds, the same animals – but now they are tainted with my fear. It dries my throat and tightens my chest. I have been across the great salt water to a new world, but I have never been so far into the wilderness.

I search my mind for what I know: that the Mangoak extract copper far away in the mountains where the River Roanoke widens and forks. It is the river that leads me on, although I keep to the trees that fringe its banks, where it is always twilight.

And always the thought of the terror tree.

Above me, the canopy is thick with vines and creepers, the home of the *manitous*, with their devil souls. I do not trust this wilderness to keep me safe. Sometimes, the enormity of what I am doing freezes me. I cannot move, although insects nip my skin. But when the moon glints on the river, the thought comes to me as it did in Plymouth. The same moon shining on us all. Tom might be looking at it now.

Each morning, the sun brings the hills closer, swelling like the sea. Clouds drift around their peaks. Sometimes, I hear the Mangoak pass close by, their laughter harsh, their tongues clicking, a feather drifting to the ground.

As the ground rises, the birch trees give way to pine. Then the ground slopes once more toward the river, where it widens, where its waters churn between enormous boulders. Darkness brings a chill that makes my teeth rattle, but I dare not light a fire. I move more quickly, until the scent of pine smoke catches in my throat. I stop.

The Mangoak are squatting around their fire. The one who touched my earrings gets up and comes to the trees where I crouch. He fumbles under his deerskin apron, and, in seconds, a stream of pee splatters the leaves, splashing my skin. He walks back to the fire. At last, when they sleep, I set off into the shadows, fearing every slipping stone, thanking the moon for its gentle glow. It must be twenty nightfalls since I left Moratoc.

Go back, I tell myself. Forget about the pale men and women. They are not meant to live in this land. Yes, go back and honor your mother's grave, for she must surely have passed to the Upper World. Beg your father's forgiveness. Marry Seekanauk.

NO. Like Master White, I have come too far to go back.

* * *

One moonless night, when the clamor of frogs covers all other sounds, I bathe in the river. As the water trickles down my forehead, I make the sign of the cross as they did to baby Virginia. But no joyful light fills me.

I breathe in a smell that I recognize from the forge – hot and metallic. I follow the river all night, praying to the gods to bring me Tom while I have the strength to move. At dawn, clouds wrap an island close to the bank, where fires flicker, and I seek the safety of the trees once more.

How shall I ever forget the sight that morning brought to me?

The rising mist reveals people squatting at the river's edge, scooping up the water with clay dishes. I cannot see them clearly from so far, but I see that their faces and limbs are brown, that they are old and young, men and women.

They tip the dishes, watching as the water drains away, peering into them and scooping again – already working although the sun has hardly risen. Others are clinging to the rocks above them, lighting fires that belch black smoke. Then, quickly, they push aside the fires with sticks and pour water onto the heated rocks. As they hiss and split, I hear them crack open. Then they light the fires again, but deeper in the cracks the fires have made.

I shiver and touch my earrings. Children no bigger than Joshua are lifting the boiling water and pushing glowing embers with sticks. The Mangoak straddle the ridges, tongues clicking, ropes lashing out.

They take captives and copper.

Fire everywhere: under pots, inside rocks, golden fire in the sky.

Popogusso.

I crawl between the boulders on the river bed, where the water is clean. I wait. It is not long before a woman and a young girl pick up water pots and trudge toward me. My heart turns over. Our women do not trudge, even if they are tired. We walk almost on the front of our feet. These people walk like pale people. Tattered cloths hide their faces.

Two Mangoak watch, nudging each other, only losing interest when their captives squat behind the biggest boulder. When they have washed, they kneel and clasp their hands together, like the people in Saint Andrew's church.

I take my chance, whispering, "Amen."

The girl, whose skin is as dark as mine, does not scream, but opens her mouth in surprise, and as the woman puts out her hand to calm her, the cloth falls from her face. The sun flickers in my eyes. A bird screeches.

Her hair is so thinned that I can see the sores on her scalp, where flies cluster. Her skin is sunburned and spotted with blisters and bites. Two of her front teeth are missing. The holes in her shift almost expose her breasts. Her hands, which refused to toil on Roanoke, are blistered. And everywhere – scalp, nostrils, nails – tinged with pale green.

"Agnes? What have they done to you?"

Her dulled eyes focus. She hides her face again. "Don't look at me!"

I swallow my tears – tears of shame because, in my need for Tom, I have almost forgotten about the ones with him: Mary, Will, Agnes, Joshua and others whose names I have already forgotten.

"Where is Tom?" Her mouth opens and closes under the cloth without a sound. "Where are the others, Agnes?"

She shows her face then, and her eyes blaze at me.

"It's your fault! You should *never* have sent us to Moratoc. We'd all be safe in Roanoke now. The supply ship would have come. We could have gone back to Plymouth." She picks up a handful of pebbles and throws them at me. The dark-skinned girl copies her. "You're a murdering savage."

My skin smarts. "The Mangoak do not usually go so far south. But the winter was severe. Perhaps they lost their captives to the cold. I do not know, Agnes. They are not my people. Please, Agnes. Where is he?"

Water gurgles in the pot. "Get away from here! Or I'll tell your vile copperheads. They'll silence you. They'll rip out that sweet-talking tongue, like they did to this poor girl." She glances down the river and laughs. "Anyhow, you won't find him here. He's dead."

My heart enters dark shadows. My lips ache to cry out.

A whistle screeches and the birds take flight. Agnes and the girl pick up the pots and walk away. But at the last minute, Agnes calls over her shoulder. "Your savages didn't even bother to bury him. They threw his body into the river, and Mary's."

The spark of hope that brought me here dies down. I stay, hidden in the rocks, hoping she will come again. I see the outline of a Mangoak, hand over his eyes, scanning the river valley. Then I am glad of my brown skin. But I do not know what to do with all my tears. My body tingles with the pain of crying, my eyes so swollen that I hardly see the sun.

I shall protect you. I shall be more use to you than a wife who can sew and bake.

I have not protected Tom. I have killed him.

Agnes returns at last light. The evening sun reddens the rocks, penetrating the clefts with shafts of light, and casting long shadows. The moon is rising. I bring myself to life, rubbing and stretching my legs.

"Will says I must tell you what happened," she begins. "We were packed up and ready to come to you, on the way to Roanoke. Tom was determined...we were still half-asleep. These…savages roped us together and, by dawn, we were on our way here." Her eyes brim. "Edward died on the way. And Master Payne."

"How did Tom die? *Tell* me!"

"Mary caught the fever first. Her bowels moved all the time, and she vomited blood. Tom did all he could. He shaded her. He gave her his water. They wouldn't even untie her. They just laughed. A white woman covered in her own filth, sickened by the stench. But she died with God's name on her lips. They were both dead in the morning..."

My heart lurches. "What was wrong with Tom?"

"I don't know. But what does it matter? They've got their own little test for the dead. We all had to form a circle to watch, even the little ones. One of them took a knife – they have plenty of them now, thanks to us – lifted Mary's little finger and chopped it off. She didn't make a sound...then it was Tom's turn...neither did he..." The sun flashes low over the hills. "Thank God my baby died at Moratoc. No, it wasn't Tom's, born before its time. Its father paid for me to leave Bideford. Thirty pieces of silver, eh? Or copper, as it turns out..." Her tongue is wild now. The girl tugs at her skirt. A whistle screeches.

My stomach is turning over. I must get away. "Come with me, Agnes."

"No, and you shouldn't ask, now that you've seen what they do to those who try to escape. I'd rather die here. And I couldn't do that to Josh and Will." She sighs. "Think of us and pray that we die soon."

"My people will help you. We can come back for you, I promise."

Her face becomes fierce. "NO. Don't use us as a cause for killing. Our lives aren't worth it now." She grips my arm. "We *want* to die."

She releases my arm, picks up the pot and walks away. I trust the river mist to keep us safe as I follow. "The terror tree!" I whisper. "Where the Mangoak hang tongues...I have not seen it. Is there such a thing?"

Agnes looks at me as if I, too, am losing my mind. "We don't need a tree to terrify us," she replies, her eyes flashing with the old taunting.

I move until dawn, keeping away from the river for fear of finding his body, making my own winding way through forested slopes stretching before me, pale green like the sea, broken only by the river and clouds of mist. I trudge like a pale woman, like Agnes and the mute girl – all lost to the wilderness.

I have nowhere to go.

The river is always in my sight, gleaming through the trees, and in my ears as it roars over the rocks. When I go to drink, I cup my hands quickly, my eyes closed.

Every day is dark. I sleep and walk whenever I choose. I circle like the Assistant until I drop. The animals keep away as they do when one of their own is wounded. A bed of moss and ferns. Sucking dew from the leaves, reaching for a wild strawberry, staining my lips and fingers.

Not enough to live. Too much to die. Neither fish nor fowl.

No Hester to bring me milk and honey.

Days drift past. My bones ache. My sharp spine settles deeper into mossy softness. Breastless chest. Shoulder blades as sharp as wings, like that night at the Plymouth waterside. My heart's shriveled like the pig's heart in the forge.

Soon I shall slip out of my skin like a snake and fly to the Upper World.

No Tom to take me home.

Old woman's hands, trembling and withered. Nails the color of grapes.

At night, my eyes follow the fireflies. Wolves bay, but their summer-filled stomachs do not need my flesh. By day, I watch the bees as they feed on honeysuckles. Their wings catch the light, like sparks from the fire. I lie in my own filth, like Mary.

Sun splashing on leaves. A splash of water and I could have been with Tom in this world.

Dust to dust, Henry used to say in the burying ground. Tom's dust will mingle with mine and we shall be part of this world forever. And the wind will carry it across the great salt water. And Hester and Henry will breathe us in.

I crawl into the cool vines where flames light my dreams. Tom is lying in front of a fire, eyes closed, skin colorless. It showers sparks into the sky like on Saint Clement's Day. Iron bars lie in the flames, their tips red-hot. Fire is magic. It can change metal. Can it change flesh? I pick up a bar, touch Tom's heart, sizzling the flesh, and he opens his eyes, reaches out for me.

Forty days and forty nights wandering in this wilderness. Like Christ, Henry said, before he died on the cross.

But who will know *my* story?

The smell of burning is so strong that I open my eyes. There is more fire in the sun today than I have ever seen. Then I see that the forest is blazing around me. Flames spit as they consume the dry forest floor, sucking in the air, leaving me gasping. They strengthen and leap, suddenly still, then leap again. Above me, vines shrivel, showering sparks. Others, ragged like birds' feathers in the dust, scorch and flare. Wild tobacco plants burn, making my head spin, and I try not to breathe deeply for it makes men as wild and as unpredictable as bears.

I am not dreaming.

The gods have chosen. *Popogusso*, my punishment for leaving my people.

But the circle of fire will take me to Tom.

Tongues of flame reach out. The fire was safe in Tom's hands. He would have saved me.

Wild pigs squeal, their flesh roasting as they run. Deer leap, their skin singeing, their tails flashing flames, their eyes fixed on the river. Some panic and run back into the fire. *All* afraid of the forest that has sheltered them.

Not a breath of air. The pit of hell.

A horse thunders past, nostrils flaring, mouth foaming with terror. Once I squatted under a silver birch tree by the lake, and asked my guiding spirit to show itself and, in my vision, I saw a creature pawing the ground in front of me, a creature the pale men call a horse. But this horse is flesh and blood. I catch hold of its tail and let it drag me, my feet skimming hot ash, my body bending under charred branches…faster than the flames...over pebbles so hot that my feet hardly touch them…until the river cools us.

A splash of water…

God. Gods. What does it matter?

Water splashes my face with such force that I open my eyes. Rain is roaring through the billowing smoke.

Lightning flashes like metal. The forest hisses, giving up its last flames as it cools, and, by the afternoon, it is as black as the sky, for smoke still shadows the sun. But I see ragged clumps of cloud for the first time that day, moving toward the hills. The pigs are grubbing among the trees, wondering where their world has gone. The horse stands still with shock. I whisper soothing words as I stroke him, until he is brave enough to leave me.

The storm has passed, filling the forest – and my heart – with a great calm. If my guiding spirit has brought me this far, I shall respect it. Strength seeps back into my body, enough to let me pick the berries overhanging the bank and scoop up water. Then I turn my back to the blackened forest. Smoke still darkens my path, but now it is thinning as it rises.

Savage. Silva. Somebody who comes from the forest. I shall go back to Moratoc. That is where I shall live until I grow strong enough to go to Roanoke, for Tom's people must be told what has happened.

I follow the river day after day, keeping my eyes fixed on the green ahead, until I come to Moratoc. It is just as I left it two moons ago, except that the houses are smothered with vines.

I am no longer afraid to go inside the house, where I rest on one of the mossy beds. I am no longer afraid to light a fire outside, although the fragments of wood that I use give flames too brief to bring me Tom's face. The fishing weirs, although they are rotting, give me as much salmon as I can eat. I prise open my marriage box, and at night, when it cools, I put on a dress, and hang yellow ribbons at the door and imagine Tom coming back, a deer across his shoulders, imagine him glancing into the cradle at my feet.

It is almost twelve moons since Tom and I came to my land, since those days on Roanoke Island. Now I must go back there without him, although I fear Master White's anger when he knows what has happened. Will he take his revenge on my people, as he did in Desamonquepeuc? I do not know, but I cannot let Tom be forgotten.

The river is shallow when I go to wash. No rain has fallen since the days of fire, and the water hardly comes to my waist where I stand. Then I crouch in dismay, for, on the opposite bank, a young man, brown-skinned and brown-haired, is walking into the water. Bright feathers spike his hair. He sinks, and the feathers bob. For a moment, I forget that he is a Mangoak, and smile, remembering that pleasure of bathing on Roanoke after all those weeks on the *Lion.* I crouch lower as he surfaces.

The sun flashes. Although his skin is brown, the man's hair is now a glorious yellow – like corn, like sunflowers, like the sun itself. I blink, but he is still there.

"Tom?" It is a long time since I spoke, and my voice is weak. I stand. "TOM," I call again.

He turns his head toward the sound. Then he is striding through the water, staring at me, like that first day in Plymouth – his green eyes smiling and unafraid. No, I cannot blink him away. He *is* alive. Now he is touching the copper at my ears and the fire leaps inside me. And I notice the little finger of his right hand is missing.

My magic man, who can rise from the dead, his wounds healed.

"*Onida,* no more," he whispers.

Glossary

firedogs – a pair of decorative metal supports for wood burning in a fireplace.

fishing weir – an enclosure of stakes set in a stream as a trap for fish.

the flux – a general term used for any disease which caused an excessive loss of fluid, e.g: dysentery which causes severe diarrhoea.

fringe – the front section of a person's hair, cut to hang over the forehead; bangs.

the Hoe – local term for the Plymouth Hoe in England, a large public space which faces south out to sea.

let his blood – an old medical practice that involved making small incisions in a patient, or applying leeches, to drain blood. It was believed this would remove sickness and disease from the body.

prentice – an old term for an apprentice.

ruffs – a tightly gathered piece of material worn at the neck, similar in appearance to a frilly collar. At the peak of their popularity, some ruffs were over thirty centimetres wide, starched stiff and supported by wire scaffolds.

smuts – the dirty marks made by particles of soot.

tiddy oggies – thick, potato-filled pastries, similar to an English Cornish pasty.

Author's Note

Some years ago, when I was researching a short book about Sir Walter Raleigh, I came across a painting of a young girl, one of many made in the sixteenth century by John White during his expeditions to the New World, arranged and financed by Raleigh. Many of these paintings survived and are still held in the British Museum.

This painting fascinated me. What could this young girl's life have been like at the meeting of two different worlds?

This was my inspiration for Nadie's story.

I learned that another attempt was made, in 1587, to colonize America, with more than a hundred English men, women and children. I was struck by the fact that, for the first time, people in England were willing to travel thousands of miles to live in a new world – possibly forever. This colony became known as "The Lost Colony", because all of them disappeared – and their fate is still unknown today.

This was my inspiration for Tom's story.

A World Away is a work of fiction, based on the 1586 and 1587 colonies in the New World. I have used the real names of the tribes already living there – but not the names of individuals, except for Chief Wingina. The cruel Mangoak tribe did exist, but the tongue torture is mine entirely. I have used the real names of the colonists, where historical detail is known, such as George Howe, who *was* murdered in the reeds – and John White's daughter, Eleanor, her husband Ananias, and their daughter, Virginia, the first English child to be born in America.

I wrote this book in memory of not only "The Lost Colony" but of all those who still live dislocated lives.

Pauline Francis

Bibliography

Brereton, John, *Discoverie of the North Part of Virginia* (16) March of America Facsimile Series, 1966

Bracken, CW, *History of Plymouth*, Underhill, 1931

Edwards, Paul (Ed.), *Equiano's Travels*, Heinemann, 1967

Folio Society, *The First Colonists: Hakluyt's Voyages to North America*, Folio Society, 1986

Hakluyt, Richard, *Virginia Richly Valued* (12), March of America Facsimile Series, 1966

Hariot, Thomas, *A Brief and True Report of the new found land of Virginia,* 1588

King, JCH, *First People, First Contacts,* British Museum Press, 1999

Lacey, Robert, *Sir Walter Raleigh,* Cardinal, 1975

Lewis, J. (Ed.), *The Mammoth Book of Native Americans,* University of North Carolina Press, 1983

Miller, Lee, *Roanoke: Solving the Mystery of England's Lost Colony,* Pimlico, 2001

Quinn, David Beers, *Set Fair for Roanoke: Voyages and Colonies, 1584-1606,* University of North Carolina Press, 1984

Sloan, Kim, *A New World: England's First View of America,* British Museum Press, 2007

Stick, David, *Roanoke Island: The Beginning of English America,* University of North Carolina Press, 1983

Taylor, Alan, *American Colonies – The Settling of North America,* Penguin, 2001

Other sources

John White's paintings at the British Museum

The Algonquian language:

Hariot, Thomas, White, John, Lawson, John, *A Vocabulary of Roanoke,* The American Language Reprint Series, Evolution Publishing, 2006

Spotted Wolf of the Snow Owl website, for the following words not found in the above:

amitola	rainbow
keegsquaw	virgin
nadie	wise one
onida	the lost one who is sought/waited for (girl use only)

Acknowledgments

I want to thank all my family for their constant interest and support, especially my daughter Anna, for her incisive comments on the manuscript. I owe enormous thanks to Megan Larkin of Usborne for leading me gently toward the deeper paths of the story. Thanks to my agent, Catherine Clarke, and to Katy, for reading the manuscript aloud for me.

And a special thanks to my childhood friend, Mr. Don Clayphan, the curator of the Old Smithy, Owston

Ferry, Lincolnshire for allowing me to visit the blacksmith's forge after hours. This is where I used to watch the blacksmith work while waiting for the school bus – and where I kept warm in winter.

Pauline Francis has worked as a school librarian and a French teacher, and spent time in Africa translating books before becoming a writer herself. She has written educational stories, such as *Sam Stars at Shakespeare's Globe*, focusing on her favorite subject, the sixteenth century, and retold classics such as *Oliver Twist*. She has also written for young people who are learning English as a foreign language. She returned to the sixteenth century in *Raven Queen*, her first novel – a tale of love and tragedy based on the life of Lady Jane Grey.

Pauline is married with two grown-up children and lives in Hertfordshire.

To find out more about Pauline Francis, visit her website: www.paulinefrancis.co.uk

Usborne Quicklinks

For links to websites where you can see paintings by John White, read more about "The Lost Colony" and see evidence of the first English settlers to arrive on the north-east coast of America, go to the Usborne Quicklinks Website at www.usborne-quicklinks.com and enter the keywords "a world away".

When using the Internet, make sure you follow the Internet safety guidelines displayed on the Usborne Quicklinks Website. Usborne Publishing is not responsible for the content on any website other than its own. We recommend that children are supervised while on the Internet, that they do not use Internet chat rooms, and that you use Internet filtering software to block unsuitable material. For more information, see the "Net Help" area on the Usborne Quicklinks website.

Usborne Publishing is not responsible and does not accept liability for the availability or content of any website other than its own, or for any exposure to harmful, offensive, or inaccurate material which may appear on the Web. Usborne Publishing will have no liability for any damage or loss caused by viruses that may be downloaded as a result of browsing the sites it recommends.

Also by Pauline Francis

Raven Queen

I have lived the life of a princess since the day I was born.
But it did not bring me what I wanted. I am still trapped.

My beloved Ned speaks of love, freedom, a future. To walk with
him in the forest, our raven soaring above us, is my only joy.
But my father plans that I shall be betrothed to the King,
and I am afraid. Queens of England have a habit of dying.
I have no desire to take the throne, no wish to
find myself in the Tower of London.

Wife, Queen – I fear it will bring me to my knees.

Raven Queen weaves a mesmerizing tale of love
and tragedy based on the life of Lady Jane Grey,
all too often remembered as just a line in a
world history book.

ISBN 9780794527556

Praise for *Raven Queen*

"Written in timeless language with a hint of the poetic in the spare prose, the book underpins the love story with thoughtful imagery and symbolism... The book has an enduring theme of religious intolerance, makes the 16th-century vivid and ends with an unforgettable twist." *The Sunday Times*

"Francis' alternating first-person narrative weaves a fascinating story." *Bookseller's Choice, The Bookseller*

"A visceral, mesmerizing debut novel...relayed through a series of thrilling, climactic tableaux in haunting, lyrical style."

TES Magazine

"An utterly fabulous read... Philippa Gregory for a younger audience." *Rachel Forward, Gardners Books*

"This stunning and lyrical tale will hold readers captive and haunt them long after the last page has been turned."

Becky Stradwick, Borders